LOVE CONQUERED

First Edition

Published by The Nazca Plains Corporation
Las Vegas, Nevada
2009

ISBN: 978-1-935509-68-4

Published by

The Nazca Plains Corporation ®
4640 Paradise Rd, Suite 141
Las Vegas NV 89109-8000

PUBLISHER'S NOTE
Love Conquered is a work of fiction created wholly by *Dan Carroll's*
imagination. All characters are fictional and any resemblance to
any persons living or deceased is purely by accident. No portion of
this book reflects any real person or events.

Cover Photo, Alvaro Pantoja
Art Director, Blake Stephens

ACKNOWLEDGEMENTS

It's hard to believe that another book is, at last, complete, but here it is in front of me so, unless I'm dreaming, it must be so, right? I've read many such anthologies in the past and kept thinking, 'Why not see what I can do myself?' And so, fingers to keyboard, I came up with some ideas for the shorts and a general theme for all of them and off I went!

I'd had the rather grandiose idea that I could get this done in a matter of weeks, but, of course, what author doesn't tell themselves that only to find that those weeks fly by and it becomes a month and then another? Fortunately, I had my wonderful support system to push and drive me to get this done and so it was only a matter of four months, which flew by sometimes faster than I hoped, from start to finish for this book.

As always, I couldn't have brought this to completion without those people who are near and dear to me and helped me through their wisdom, guidance, help and assistance and they are, to me, my angels who keep me going and motivated. And those angels would be:

Dan E.: I know I've told you this so many times before, but you were instrumental in getting me started in this crazy world we call writing and I've never regretted it for one moment. You're always there to be my sounding board and to listen to me rant and rave when I'm stuck and I hope I've been able to return the favor equally. And you should know how much I appreciate those flashes of brilliance you shot at me that spurred some of the ideas from which these stories sprang. You were truly the oil for me when my hinges became rusty...and you knew I couldn't resist that, didn't you?

My family: Each and every day I thank whatever gods there are that all of you are in my life and being there for me with all the love and support you had to give. You all know that you have a very, very special place in my heart. And especially to you, MR, for pushing and prodding me toward the end of this book, especially those times when I was so stuck and had no idea about where to go next. I know I've already said this to you in person, but your observation and brilliant suggestion concerning the last part of the book was a godsend to me and I can only hope that you know how much that meant to me.

Dedication

FOR RICK, MICHAEL, BRAD, AND DAN
MY REAL-LIFE ANGELS!

LOVE CONQUERED

First Edition

Dan Carroll

Contents

The Final Test   1

The Beach House   15

Forbidden Love   23

Lovin' Country   31

Over Your Shoulder   41

Forever Yours   49

A Meeting Of Minds   55

Boys and Men   67

Blue and Grey   81

Needs Of A Friend   91

Loving Your Enemy   101

Never Farther Than Your Front Door   109

Under The Waves   123

The Escape   131

About The Author   139

The Final Test

The last thing he remembered, he was in the locker room at the college gym and was finishing toweling his hair dry when he suddenly had the feeling he wasn't alone. Before he had time to react, however, he found his arms hammered behind him and a cloth placed over his nose and mouth. The smell of the chloroform was the last memory he had until he came to just now.

Mike still felt the bitter taste of chloroform in his mouth as he came to, opening his eyes slowly. Looking around, he saw nothing but pitch black as his still-groggy mind tried to clear. Realizing his arms were up in the air, he attempted to bring them down and suddenly realized that they were chained to a high bar attached to the dark ceiling overhead.

Looking down, his breath caught as he realized his 6'2", 190 pound muscular-defined body was stripped down to his briefs, his toes just barely touching the floor. As he flexed his powerful arms fastened tightly to the overhead bar, his mind raced as he tried to figure out why he was here and who had brought him here.

Sweat began to run down from his forehead and underarms as he yelled out, "Hey! Anybody here? Let me out of here! This isn't funny!" His voice echoed off the dark walls in response.

His eyes adjusted to the darkness and he sucked in air again as he saw the various objects and implements hanging from the walls all around him. Paddles, floggers, chains, whips and other paraphernalia surrounded him as he realized he was bound in the center of the room.

Looking from left to right as best he could, he saw the leather sling, bondage table and St. Andrews cross, realizing that he was being held captive in a dungeon. Where he was, he had no idea. His only thought being that he had to find some way to get free and escape.

The leather restraints strapped and locked around his wrists began to bite into them as he struggled harder, hoping against hope that he could somehow pull the chains loose. Even as he struggled, his briefs had begun to bulge as his manhood filled with blood and expanded within them, his testicles full and tight as well.

He had fantasized many times about just this kind of situation, of being bound and chained and worked over, but he had never told anyone about the kinds of things he dreamed about as he jerked off at night in his dorm room. After all, he was the captain of the college football team and wrestling team and was one of the straightest guys anyone had ever seen. He had several on-again, off-again relationships with many of the girls on campus, but somehow they never seemed to satisfy him the way that his masturbatory fantasies did.

He called out again, louder this time, hearing his own deep voice bounce off the walls. Whoever had brought him here obviously had some twisted ideas and planned to keep him waiting as long as possible.

A sudden thought came to Mike's mind as he grinned and thought to himself "Oh wait...this is probably just a joke. I bet Tom and Jack are behind this. Those two jokers are always pulling shit like this." Calling out again, he yelled, "OK, you guys! You got me! You can come out now and let me go!"

Again, there was no response other than the muscular jock's voice bouncing off the walls. Sure of the fact that this was all just a practical joke being played on him, Mike stopped struggling against the chains and began to breathe easier. Suddenly, he thought of his latest girlfriend, Stacy, and started to laugh as he wondered what she'd say if she were to walk in and see him strung up like this.

His laughter echoed off the walls at that, and then suddenly stopped as he heard the sounds of three pairs of feet overhead, walking around. Judging from the sound, he guessed that whoever the three were, they were wearing heavy boots. He could barely make out the faint sound of muffled voices, but couldn't understand what was being said.

He yelled out again for his friends and the voices stopped for a moment, then the sound of a man's voice came from a small speaker at the top of the opposite wall. The deep voice said, "Welcome to my web, boy. We've been watching you for quite some time and have decided that it is time for your initiation into our brotherhood." Pausing for a moment, Mike felt the sweat begin to run again as the voice continued, "We know that you will make a good addition to our group...once, you have been properly broken and trained, that is."

A cold chill ran down the college jock's spine at that last comment, his lightly-hairy body sweating harder. The voice spoke again. "We will be with you soon, boy. You will learn and know what it is to serve men when we are done with you. Until then, I suggest you relax. You cannot escape, however, should you attempt such, let me assure you that you would not see the light of day again as punishment."

A deep, demonic laugh came from the speaker as it was shut off. A pool of sweat had formed on the rubber matted floor under Mike's feet as he flexed his arms, trying again to break the chains and get loose. Still considering that this was all just a joke, somewhere deep inside his mind, he knew two things. Whoever these men were, they were not joking and they had somehow discovered the secret fantasies that he held within his mind.

The muffled voices overhead began again as their boots moved across the floor. Mike stopped struggling for a moment as, suddenly, candles lit up on the sconces hanging on the wall. The jock wondered how candles light themselves when there was no one there but him as he looked around the darkened room, able to see the objects and equipment clearer now.

As he pivoted his head back and forth, he finally felt the leather that surrounded his neck and realized that he had already been collared. His cock twitched again from this and he could feel some precum leaking out into his tight briefs and his breathing becoming short gasps.

If it had not been for the threatening tone of the deep voice earlier, Mike somehow knew deep down inside that he could and would get off on the situation, but the voice had threatened his life if he attempted to escape and that made the jock scared and nervous as he hung there in the center of the dungeon.

His muscular biceps were very strong and tight, but the blood flow to them had been somewhat arrested and were starting to go numb. He manage to grab onto the chains with both hands and pulled his body up, bending his elbows as he tried to get the blood pumping again.

As he pulled himself up higher and higher toward the ceiling, he suddenly realized that he was close to a horizontal bar attached to the ceiling. With a grin, he saw that the bar was not metal but some kind of a very thick hardwood. If he could just pull up higher, maybe he could grab the bar and somehow break it or dislodge it from the ceiling.

His biceps trembling as the muscles flexed and popped out, he had almost gotten to within hands grasp of it when he remembered the threat from earlier. Still, if he could get loose, at least that would give him an advantage. Mike wasn't sure how many men there were, but if he weren't chained up, he felt sure he could take them on and escape before they could carry out that ominous threat.

Determination coursed through him as he saw the bar within his reach and, holding onto a chain with his right hand, he reached up, his left hand grabbing onto the thick wood bar. Suddenly, he yelled out in pain as an electric current shot out from the bar into his hand, down his muscled arm and down his left side.

The current stopped suddenly as Mike lost his grip on both the bar and the chain and fell back toward the floor, the chains attached to the leather restraints around his wrists stopping his descent suddenly. His arms were on fire as they felt as though they had been dislocated as he hung there with his head down toward his muscled chest.

Opening his eyes slowly, he realized that the current had been a warning and was not powerful enough to kill, but the jolt had weakened him enough that he knew that he would be unable to try it again. Frustration, anger and worry began to set in as his mind slowly started to accept the fact that he was trapped with no means of escape.

Would these faceless, nameless men only use him for their own twisted pleasure? The deep voice had said that he had been chosen to join their brotherhood. Somehow, Mike knew that this was not part of some fraternity pledge initiation. Was he still somewhere on campus? There were no windows in this room, leading the jock to think he was in the basement of a building.

As time crawled slowly by, the muscled jock felt the thirst building in his throat as the sweat continued to run off his body like a river onto the floor. How long had he been here? Hours? Days? How long would they keep him here before they revealed themselves? What would they do with and to him once they began? The books and stories that Mike had read during his private jack off sessions told of men and boys who had been captured and used and abused in many brutal and torturous ways. But, that was all fiction and fantasy, wasn't it? That kind of thing didn't happen in real life, after all. Or, did it?

As the muscled jock's mind dealt with all these questions, suddenly the sound of the booted feet got louder, then stopped nearby. A key was inserted into a lock and turned. A faint stream of light came through the door as the three figures entered, the last of them closing and locking the door behind him.

The three men were all powerfully-built and dressed in leather from head to toe, their faces covered by hoods. Mike's eyes widened at the size of the three men and his heart sank as he realized that even if he could get loose, he was no match for these three powerhouses. At the same time, his cock and balls twitched hard inside his briefs at the thought of what these three men had planned for the jock's initiation.

Mike watched as his three captors moved quietly around the room without uttering a sound. They began taking some of the objects from the walls and laying them out on a small table nearby.

The largest of the three came toward the jock. Judging that the man had to be at least 6'4" and approximately 265 pounds, Mike attempted to make eye contact with the man when, suddenly, a full head leather hood was slipped on and tied closed behind his head. With no openings for his eyes, Mike began to breathe faster, but realized that there were openings for both his nose and a zippered opening for his mouth.

The big man moved away after securing the hood, returning to his companions. With the hood also covering his ears, Mike couldn't hear much as the men moved around the room. As he hung there, the college jock suddenly felt the open neck of a bottle against his lips and a deep voice command, "Drink, boy." The water poured into his mouth and he swallowed it down gratefully as his thirst was, at last, quenched.

The bottle was removed and he was left there, hanging by his arms. Moments later, a deep, gruff voice said, "Now, we begin..."

=================

Vague, wild images swam through Mike's mind as he dreamed deeply. Huge, muscular men in leather...whips...chains...his body being used and abused by these faceless men again and again. He could hear his howls and gasps of both pain and pleasure as these men took him to heights that he had never known before.

Suddenly, the jock yelled out loudly, waking himself up. His eyes opened slowly and he felt the cool wash of sweat all over his body as he tried to raise up. The last thing he remembered was being bound and chained in that dungeon, his captors working every part of his body hard and rough.

As his eyes opened completely, the light coming through a window made him squint and he realized he was no longer in the dungeon, but in a large bed somewhere. Mike struggled to sit up, looking down at himself and saw the single sheet covering his sweaty body, realizing that he was naked underneath it. And, he was not bound to the bed.

His mind racing, he wondered just how long he'd been in the dungeon and how long he'd been here in this room, wherever it was. He sat up in the bed and tried to look out through the window, but it was covered with curtains preventing him from seeing anything outside that might give him a clue as to where he was.

Suddenly feeling exhausted, he laid his head back down on the pillow underneath it and suddenly smiled to himself as he struggled to remember what had happened in that dungeon. He could feel that nothing was broken, even though his muscles were sore and aching from the workout he'd been put through.

Taking some deep breaths, he sat up again, pulling the sheet aside and swinging his muscled legs over the side. On a small table beside the bed sat a large bottle of water and Mike grabbed it and, opening it, took some large gulps of it, feeling the cool liquid flow inside him, quenching his thirst.

Standing up, he sat the bottle down on the table and moved to the window and pushed the curtains aside, determined to find out where he was. Unfortunately, the glass was covered in reflective Mylar that only showed his image reflected back. Mike grabbed the window sill, trying to open it but found that it was securely locked. Whoever these men were, they had made sure that he could not discover where he had been brought.

Examining the room, the jock saw the door and went over to it, trying it but already knowing that it was probably locked as well. Finding that it was, he looked down at his naked frame again and suddenly wished that he had something to put on to cover himself. Not that he had anything against being bareassed. He'd spent many nights just this way alone in his private dorm room as he made love to his own body and let himself get lost in his personal fantasies. But, that was different. He had control of the situation then and now, somehow, he knew that he was no longer in charge of his own destiny.

As he moved around the room, he discovered a second door, but on opening it, he found that it contained a small bathroom. At least these men had made sure he would be able to take care of any personal needs. Going inside, he found soap and towels and quickly took a shower, washing the musky smell of his own body off. In the shower, his hands began soaping up his muscled body. Suddenly, his fingers ran across his nipples and cock and, shaking the water from his eyes, he looked down to find the silver rings going through both of his thick nipples as well as the metal ring hanging from the head of his cock. He had no memory of how these piercings had gotten there, but something about them was a turn-on for him as he cleaned his body. As he dried off and stepped from the shower, his eyes fell on a small table and saw the black leather shorts laying there.

Smiling to himself, he slipped the shorts on over his legs, pulling them up around his waist and fastening them closed. Mike stepped out of the small bathroom and walked back to the window, stretching his arms out over his head. As he saw his reflection looking back at him, his mouth fell open as he finally saw the metal ring encircling his neck. He remembered the leather collar that had been around it from the night before, but evidently that had been changed at some point by the men.

Examining the circle of metal, he discovered that there was no catch or release to remove it, only a small Allen screw on one side of it. Mike knew that the men had the wrench that could open it and also knew they weren't about to freely give it him. He turned away from the window as he fingered the metal collar and heard the sound of something being opened. He moved across the room just in time to see a small panel open in the door and a tray inserted through it. A deep voice said, "Good morning, brother. We thought you might be hungry. Take this and eat. We will be coming for you again, soon."

Somehow, Mike knew better than to try and knock the tray away and reach through the opening to grab at whoever was on the other side. Taking the tray, the panel was quickly closed and locked back. The jock looked at the tray and saw the food, suddenly feeling ravenously hungry. Taking the tray over to the bed, he sat down and eagerly ate the provided food, washing it down with more of the bottled water.

Feeling better now that he'd cleaned up and eaten, he sat the tray down on the table and laid back on the bed, wondering what these men had in store for him. Suddenly, he realized what the voice of the man on the other side of the door had said. He had called him "brother", not "boy". Did that mean than he had passed the initiation they had put him through last night or was there more to come that he didn't know about, yet?

Almost as if someone had heard his thoughts, he heard a key in the lock of the door turn. He remained laying on the bed, unsure if he should get up to greet whoever it was coming in. As the door opened, Mike saw the man from last night, obviously the leader of the group, enter and come over to the bed. He was dressed this morning in a leather harness and the same shorts that the jock wore as well as a pair of leather boots. Over his face, there was a half mask covering the upper part of his head.

"Stand up, brother. It is time," the man said. Mike obeyed as he swung his legs over the side of the bed and got to his feet. The masked man brought a hand up and quickly covered the top half of the jock's head in the same mask that he wore, fastening it closed. It was then that Mike saw that this man wore the same metal collar around his neck and had both nipples pierced as well.

The man said nothing more as he led the jock to the doorway and through it. They moved down a long hallway then stopped at a pair of double doors. Opening one of the doors, his masked companion led him through it and closed and locked it behind them. Mike looked around the room, dimly-lit by candles as the dungeon had been. As his eyes adjusted to the light, he saw ten other men standing there in a semi-circle, attired the same as he and the man beside him were.

One of the other men moved forward, saying, "Is he ready for the final test?" His companion nodded his head as he moved away to stand with the other men. The eleventh man came forward, holding an identical pair of leather boots and a leather chest harness that all of them were wearing. Staring hard into Mike's eyes, he said, "This is the final test for you. Succeed and these will be yours and you will be welcomed into our brotherhood. Failure is not an option. Do you understand?"

Mike felt all of the men's eyes on him as he slowly nodded and said, "Yes...I understand."

The man holding the harness and boots moved away, nodding to the others. Two of the other men came forward, one of them unfastening the leather shorts on the jock's body, letting them fall down his legs to his feet. Then, both of them grabbed one of Mike's muscular arms, pulling them away from his body as they turned him around, his back to the others. The voice of his companion called out, "Begin!"

Before Mike could understand or realize what was going to happen, he felt the first strikes of the floggers lash out at his back, making him gasp out loud and suck in his breath. The men holding his arms had a tight grip on him as they held him in place. As the floggers struck his muscular back and exposed ass, he could hear the leader of the group calling out, "5...6...7..."

The jock stood there taking the strikes, trying his best to endure the attack from these men. Somewhere, deep inside of him, something told him that he was changing...growing...becoming different. As the leader got to the number thirteen, the flogger hitting him stopped. Mike gulped in mouthfuls of air, wondering if this test was over. Suddenly, he felt another flogger strike his back and ass and the leader began counting again.

Without knowing how or why, the muscled jock realized that each of the men was going to have a turn at him with the flogger, thirteen times each. His moans and gasps rose and fell in volume as each of the men there flogged him. The two holding him by his arms were replaced by two others as they, too, took their turns working him over.

For what seemed like an eternity, Mike's only focus was dealing with the pain of the flogger striking his back over and over. Finally, sweat pouring off his face and body, the leader counted "13" as the last man finished his turn. The room grew quiet as the jock found himself turned back around to face his attackers. His back and ass were stinging from the strikes, but he forced himself to stand before them as the two men holding his arms released him at last, letting his arms fall to his sides.

Coming forward, the leader held out the harness and boots, saying, "It is complete. You have passed the final test, my brother. You are now one of us. Welcome to the Brotherhood of Thirteen." Setting the boots down, he indicated that Mike was to put them on. The jock bent down and shoved his bare feet into the boots, feeling the stinging on his back as he did so. As Mike stood up again, the leader came forward and put the leather harness around Mike's upper body, snapping it closed. The smell of the new leather assailed the jock's nose as he felt a tugging in his crotch.

The leader stepped back and smiled for the first time as he said, "You are now one of us. For the rest of your life. You have completed the circle." Moving toward Mike, he hugged the man against him in greeting. The jock hugged the leader back, a sudden, strong feeling of belonging washing over him like nothing he had ever felt before.

As the hug was broken, the leader snapped his fingers, calling forward two of the other men and said, "Now, you must return to where you came from, brother." Mike started to open his mouth to ask a question, but the leader held up one hand, meaning for him to be silent. "There will be time for answers to your questions later. When you are needed again, we will come for you. Be prepared and ready, brother."

Mike had no time to process this information as suddenly he smelled the strong odor of chloroform again as a rag was placed over his mouth and everything started to go dark again.

━━━━━━━━

The jock came to with a sudden start as he sat up in his bed, realizing that he was back in his private dorm room, alone. Shaking his head to bring himself more awake, he looked around the room as he said aloud, "What the hell? What a fucking dream! Was it real or was it all my imagination?" Remembering something suddenly, he looked down at his naked body to find that the mask, harness, shorts, jock and collar had been removed from his body. He got off of his bed and looked down at his chest and cock. The piercings were there, intact.

Still unsure whether any of it had been real or not, he stumbled into his bathroom. Splashing water on his face from the sink to wake himself up completely, he glanced down at his legs and sucked in his breath as he saw that on his upper right thigh was tattooed the number "13".

A Boner Book

The Beach House

The afternoon rain beat down in sheets obscuring the ocean view as Tom collapsed on the sofa with relief. "Finally done," he said to himself as he surveyed his surroundings and smiled. The last week had been a blur for him ever since he'd closed on his beach house and started moving in.

Ever since he could remember, he'd always wanted to live at the ocean and he had finally realized that dream. For months he had looked at house after house, liking bits and pieces of each one, but feeling that none of them were what he was looking for. Finally, three weeks ago, he and the agent showing him properties were driving by when Tom suddenly said, "Stop! That's it!"

The agent backed up and pulled up to the house. As they got out, the agent looked up the information on the property on his laptop and said, "Tom, we can look at it, but it's not in the best of shape. It's been empty for almost twenty years, ever since the last occupant died here."

Tom grinned and replied, "They died here? In the house? Hmmm...the perfect house and a history to it as well? I like it! In fact, I love it!"

Shaking his head at his client, the agent removed the keys from the lockbox and unlocked the front door. The two men entered the house together looking around. It was evident that the place had not been occupied for a long time. Scattered pieces of old, broken furniture sat around on the floor, paint peeling on the walls as well as a couple of broken windows gave it the feeling of a place that was ready for demolition and not for occupancy.

The agent said, "This is going to take a helluva lot of work, Tom. Are you sure this is what you're looking for?"

His client roamed around the one floor interior, examining everything in the living room, kitchen, bedroom and bathroom, mentally making notes and comparing it with the vision he had in his mind. Coming back to the agent, he said, "This is exactly what I'm looking for, Pete. Yeah, it's going to take some work, but once I'm done, you won't recognize the place."

Pete smiled and said, "Well, OK. Let's head back to my office and we can draw up the papers and submit your offer." The two men locked up the house and got back in the car.

As they drove away, Tom looked back at the house and, for a second, thought he saw someone looking at them from the large picture window on the front. Turning to Pete, he said, "You said it's been empty for twenty years, right?"

"That's right," said the agent. "Why?"

Pete looked back again at the house, but nobody was there at the window this time. "Oh, no reason. It is the perfect house, too. Just what I've been looking for! I can't wait to take ownership, fix it up and move in."

═══════════════

Now, as he sat on the sofa sipping a cup of coffee, Tom looked around at all the hard work that he and the hired contractors had done. He'd looked up the history of the beach house and found that it had been built in the 1920s during the heyday of Hollywood when all the major stars owned these kinds of places. He'd found the original blueprints and some old photos of what it had looked like then and had successfully restored it to its former glory.

As he sat there relaxing, a warm fire blazing in the large fireplace before him, Tom found his mind wandering as he tried to imagine the people that had lived there and the kinds of lives they'd led. He came to, suddenly, realizing that he must have dozed off. Then, he heard someone knocking on the front door. Smiling, he said to himself, "I bet it's Pete come to see the grand unveiling." Tom heard the rain still coming down outside as he went to the front door and opened it.

Instead of his agent, Tom found himself staring into the eyes of the most beautiful man he'd ever seen in his life. About six feet tall and a lanky 175 pounds with golden blond hair and the deepest blue eyes he'd ever seen, Tom finally found his voice after the man said, "I'm sorry to intrude upon you, but my car broke down about a mile down the road and I was wondering if I might use your telephone?"

Realizing that the man was soaking wet from the rain, Tom replied, "Oh, yes, of course. I'm sorry. Please, come in. You must be half-chilled from the rain."

The stranger smiled widely as he said, "Only just about. It figures that the one day I go out without an umbrella, this would happen." Tom could only stand there and stare as the man said, "Now, if you would be so good as to get me a towel to wipe my face and your telephone, I'll call someone to come and get me. I don't want to hold you up any longer than need be."

Finally snapping out of his trance, Tom smiled back and said, "Of course. Hang on, I'll get you a towel, then you can use the phone." Moving quickly to the bathroom, he handed the handsome man the towel as he said, "Could I get you a cup of coffee or tea or something?"

The man smiled and said, "That would be wonderful. Coffee, if you don't mind. Nothing in it. Just black."

Tom grabbed his empty mug, saying, "Be right back." He returned moments later, handing one of the steaming mugs to the stranger as the man stood there, dripping water on the wood floors and looking around at the interior.

Taking the mug, the stranger sipped at it and said, "Quite a nice place you have here. Very much in keeping with the times, I'd say." Turning to Tom, the man said, "Pardon me, where are my manners? My name is Alfred van Rittenhouse. Who's home do I have the pleasure of intruding into like a lost waif?"

Tom shook the extended hand, replying, "I'm Tom McKay. I just finished completing the renovations on the house. And, please, you aren't intruding, Mr. Rittenhouse."

The man said, "I'm very pleased to meet you, Tom, may I call you Tom? You can call me Al, if you prefer. Most people I know call me Alfred, but that seems so rather formal, don't you think?"

Sipping at his coffee, Tom said, "Well, look...Al...this rain has been coming down most of the day. Would you like to get out of those wet clothes and let them dry? I've got a robe you could borrow until your clothes dry."

Smiling widely, Al replied, "That would be wonderful, Tom. I don't particularly like the idea of catching a cold in these wet things. But, the telephone first, if you don't mind."

Nodding, Tom replied, "Oh yeah, right! The phone. It's over there on the secretary."

As Al moved to the phone, suddenly a large bolt of lightning and a loud clap of thunder boomed outside, making Tom think the situation was almost like one of those old time classic movies he loved watching. The man lifted the receiver and listened, a frown coming across his handsome face. Replacing there receiver back, he said, "How unfortunate. The telephone seems to be out of order. It must have been that lightning just now."

Tom replied, "I'm sure it'll be fixed soon. While we wait, why don't you get out of those wet clothes. There's a robe in the bathroom you can wear."

Al smiled again as he said, "Thank you so much, Tom. You are a very gracious host and I appreciate you allowing me to barge in here and disrupt you like this." As he moved into the bathroom, he said, "I won't be a moment."

Tom moved over to the fireplace and stoked the fire more, making it blaze up, then sat their mugs on the coffee table in front of the sofa. As he sat down, the door to the bathroom opened as Al came out clad in a large white terry cloth robe, his wet clothes over one arm. Tom got up and took the wet things from him and laid them out on the large hearth in front of the fire.

Turning back to his guest, Tom said, "Please, have a seat. Your clothes should be dry soon and then maybe the phone will be working again."

Al smiled at him as he sat on the sofa, pulling the robe around him with more than a little modesty. Tom could tell that although the man was lanky, he was also well-built and had the kind of body that most men would envy. He could feel a stirring in his crotch and grabbed one of the large pillows on the sofa and placed it in his lap to cover up.

The two men sat there in silence watching the fire as they sipped their coffee. Finally, Tom said, "You know, Al, you remind me of somebody, but I can't remember who."

Al grinned and blushed as he replied, "I had been wondering when you would say that, Tom. However, I think I won't jog your memory just yet. I prefer to remain a bit of a mystery for the moment."

Tom smiled back and said, "Oh gosh, I'm sorry. I didn't mean to put you on the spot like that. I'm prying and that's rude. Please accept my apology."

Waving a hand in the air, Al said, "No offense taken at all, my friend. I just prefer to remain incognito, as it were, for now, anyway."

Getting up to stoke the fire again, Tom asked, "Well, could I freshen your coffee for you? And, would you like something to eat? It looks like this rain's not gonna let up for awhile."

Al smiled again. "That would be lovely, Tom. But, don't go to a lot of trouble just for me."

"Oh, no trouble at all. I was just going to make myself a sandwich. I'm afraid all I've got at the moment is ham and cheese, if that's OK?" replied Tom as he took the mugs and went to the kitchen.

"That sounds excellent," replied Al, as he got up from the sofa and followed his host into the kitchen. "But please, allow me to help you, Tom."

Tom replied, "No, you're the guest Al. It won't take me a minute to get these ready." As he turned his back to the handsome man and started to make the sandwiches, suddenly Tom felt two arms snake around his waist. Then, the feel of a tongue and lips at his neck. "What th...ohhhhhh goddddd" said Tom as he moved back against Al.

The man said as he kissed and nuzzled Tom's neck, "I thought perhaps that you and I were kindred souls, my friend." Without waiting for a response, Al turned his host so they were face to face and kissed him hard and passionately as he held the two of them close against each other. Tom returned the kiss and held onto his guest just as tightly as the two men moved together from the kitchen, the sandwiches forgotten, toward the bedroom.

Several hours later, Tom awoke in his bed. He rolled over under the covers, one hand reaching out for the other occupant. His hand found only empty space bringing him awake suddenly. Sitting up in the bed, he looked around the bedroom and was disappointed to find that Al was not there. He got out of the bed and pulled on a pair of sweatpants and went into the living room.

The fire was still glowing with embers, the mugs were still sitting on the coffee table. However, Al's clothes were gone, replaced with the terry cloth robe, neatly folded on the hearth with a note placed on top of it. Suddenly, Tom realized that the rain had stopped and the moon had come out, shining down and through the windows. Tom took the note and read it out loud.

"Dear Tom,

Thank you ever so much for the wonderful hospitality and for allowing me to intrude upon you. You are a very wonderful man and a marvelous host and I will always remember your kindness to me."

As Tom read the last part of the note, his mouth fell open.

"Please enjoy your new home. It is so full of wonderful memories and it is just as I remember it when it was first built.

As ever, your friend,

Al"

Tom stood there, dumbstruck for a moment. "What the hell?" Rushing to the telephone, he lifted the receiver. Hearing the dial tone, he quickly dialed Pete's office phone.

The agent answered on the second ring, saying, "Hello?"

Tom almost yelled into the phone but caught himself as he said, "Pete? Remember you told me the last occupant lived here twenty years ago?"

Pete replied, "Yeah? So?"

Tom said, "Do you remember what the guy's name was?"

The agent said, "Yeah, I think, but let me check something. Hang on." He put the phone down and Tom could hear papers being looked through in the background. Pete picked the phone back up and said, "Yeah, here it is. The last occupant that lived there died back in 1975. He was an old silent film actor. Guy by the name of Van Rittenhouse. Yeah, that's him. Alfred Van Rittenhouse."

Forbidden Love

As Joey stepped off the back porch of his parents' large mansion, his eyes adjusted to the dark. He looked around to make sure no one was around, quietly closing the door behind him. His bare feet moved through the grass as he made his way across the lawn. Glancing back over his shoulder, he saw that all the lights were out in the house and nervously quickened his pace.

The large barn loomed toward him in the shadows as he could hear himself breathing in and out. As he got to the side of the barn, he looked around again to make sure no one had seen him or followed him. Stopping as he got to the large, open window, he slowed his breathing down, afraid that any sound would be overheard and would give him away.

At twenty years of age and a tall 5'10" and 180 pounds, Joey Randolph was the picture of the quintessential all-American boy, a product of the Deep South family he belonged to. His parents were well-known and loved by everyone in the town. His father was descended from over three generations of Randolphs and his mother came from two generations of Pattersons. He and his two younger brothers and sister were respected and well-liked by everyone who met them.

Even though this was the 1930's, he and his family had the best of everything that money and power could buy. Even the Great Depression had had very little effect on them, since their wealth came from the good investments that had been made in oil and farming. The estate employed nearly one hundred people, household staff, farm workers as well as two families of slaves that had been with the Randolphs for nearly two hundred years. All of those who were employed by the family were devoted to them and could not imagine a life without being there.

Even so, there were very distinct and drawn lines and rules that clearly separated the Randolphs from their employees. It was considered unthinkable that anyone would ever violate these rules and no one had ever dared attempt it.

As Joey hunched down below the window above him, he could hear his father's voice reciting his number one rule in his head. "Ah love 'n respect all them people who work for me, but they know their place as much as we know ours. Ah will never allow a Randolph to fraternize or befriend anybody who works here. It just wouldn't be right." The young man remained crouched down as he half-smiled to himself, imagining what his family would say if they knew he was here and why he was here under cover of darkness.

Just then, he heard the sound of a door opening and closing above him. Then, the sound of a bathtub being run. Joey felt a tingling sensation between his legs as he slowly and quietly raised his head to peek through the open window. The humming of an old South hymn came wafting through as the young man took in a breath and nearly gasped out loud at what he saw.

The object of his attention removed his dirty work clothes, dropping them in a pile on the floor, then climbed into the steaming tub. A deep-voiced "Ahhhhhh" came through the window as Joey watched in earnest, his right hand dropping down to squeeze the boner pressing against the inside of his pants.

Inside the bathroom, Thaddeus Washington let his dark body relax in the hot water, his sore muscles loosening up from the day of hard work. He stopped humming as he said to himself, "This here water sure feels mighty good. Ah cain't wait to get myself into bed 'n have me a good long sleep. Lawd, ah earnt mah salary fo' today, thass fo' sure." He grabbed the bar of lye soap from the basket on the wall and began rubbing it across his skin, washing away the dirt, grime and sweat from his body.

Joey's eyes watched as the man worked the soap into his smooth, dark flesh. The young man had been coming out almost every night to watch Thaddeus. As long as he could remember, the man had fascinated him. The forty-year-old black man stood 6'3" and weighed nearly 240 pounds, but all of it was hardened muscle from working on the estate. At first, Joey thought his fascination was born of just admiration for the way the man worked. Indeed, he was one of the hardest working men that the Randolphs had and he was one of the few there that Joey's family praised with compliments.

Thaddeus appreciated the praise, but never let the words go to his head. He appreciated what it meant to have a good place to live, a good job and food to eat. He thanked the Lord everyday for his good fortune and did the best job he possibly could for his employers. He was so well-liked and respected by Mr. and Mrs. Randolph that when they had to go out of town, they enlisted Thaddeus' help in looking after their children as they were growing up. The other kids liked him, but not as much as Joey. Even that first time they were left with the big black man, he seemed to take a special liking to the young man who he called "Mister Joe". Even though their father frowned on them befriending the help, the young man had pleaded and cajoled the black man into letting him help with some of the chores from time to time. Always careful and watchful, Thaddeus would let Joey help him when the other kids weren't around or playing in the house.

Before long, both of them felt the friendship they'd struck together, but as Thaddeus told him, "You 'n me got to be careful, Mister Joe. You know yo daddy wouldn't like it if he caught you helpin' me with mah chores." Because of the man's watchful eye, nobody had ever caught Joey and he working together.

More than once while they were working alongside each other, Thaddeus caught the young man watching him intently, especially if he had his shirt off. Joey watched every muscle as it flexed beneath the dark skin. The black man would just grin at the young man, wondering what he found so fascinating about watching him, but somehow knowing that it was more than just a passing fancy. When he'd catch Joey watching him with his eyes, the black man would playfully scold him with "You must have somethin' better to do than watchin' me work, Mister Joe." The young man would blush and grin, causing Thaddeus to chuckle deeply and shake his head.

As Joey grew into manhood, he began to realize that his admiration and interest in Thaddeus was more than that. Many nights he'd be alone in his room and jack off while picturing the muscular black man in his mind. His fantasies included the two of them working side by side completely bareassed, a dream that never failed to make Joey shoot. The young man came to realize that he was not like the rest of his family and yearned and dreamed about the day when he could be with and love another man. He also knew that the man he would love would be a black man, even though he knew how forbidden that was here in the Deep South. Even a white woman would never dare attempt to love a black man and vice versa. Another of those "rules" that Joey came to wonder about. If love could conquer all, then what was wrong with the feelings he had? Even though he had never been with another person in that way, Joey knew what he needed and wanted and was determined that he would make it happen someday.

As Thaddeus soaped up his dark body, Joey raised his head a little higher to watch. He licked his lips as he admired and watched the man's body in the water, his bulge throbbing harder. He could feel the front of his pants getting wet with precum as he squeezed at his crotch. His mind racing, Joey made his decision. This was who he wanted and he intended to make it happen tonight. How he didn't know, but the feeling was so all-consuming that he had to try, even at the risk of being caught.

The black man finished soaping up and settled back down into the hot water, letting his body relax and soak as he exhaled happily. Joey smiled as he watched this, then lowered himself back down and moved quietly around toward the entrance to the large barn. Opening the door as noiselessly as he could, the young man knew the way to the bathroom from memory. As he stood outside the closed door, he could hear Thaddeus' deep moans of relaxation. Looking around again but knowing that no one else was in the barn, Joey quickly stripped off his clothes, his hard cock bouncing into view.

Taking a long, deep breath, he reached for the doorknob to the bathroom and turned it. The door opened silently and he quickly entered the room, closing the door back. Thaddeus lay in the tub with his back to the young man, soaking peacefully and quietly in the hot water. Joey reached for a towel lying on the shelf and wrapped it around his waist, but his hard cock made the towel stick out the front like a tent.

Just then, the muscular black man sat up in the water, a feeling that he was not alone suddenly coming over him. As he turned, he said, "Who's there?" His eyes widening as he saw the young man standing there wearing only a towel, Thaddeus stammered out, "Mister Joe? What you doin' here? Does you need somethin'?"

Joey smiled widely as Thaddeus' eyes fell down to the front of the tented towel around the young man's waist. The black man raised his eyes again, meeting Joey's and said, "Mister Joe? I don't think you wanna be here." Standing up in the tub, Thaddeus pulled out the stopper, letting the water empty out as he grabbed another towel wrapping it around his waist. He moved toward the young man. "Now, you just git yourself back on to the big house. If yo' daddy knew you was here, he wouldn't like it one…"

Before he could finish, Joey moved forward toward him, wrapping his arms around the man's waist and pulling the two of them together. Caught off guard, the black man said, "What you doin', boy? What you…" The young man reached up, grabbing Thaddeus by the back of his head and pulled it down, their lips coming together as Joey kissed the black man deeply and passionately.

The muscular black man gasped deeply as the young man held onto him tightly, finally managing to break the kiss and push him back a few steps. Looking into his eyes, Thaddeus said, "Now, Mister Joe? This ain't right…you know that. You know I likes you 'n all, but two men ain't s'posed to be doin' nothin' like this. Yo' daddy would hang both of us in a second if he caught us."

Joey stood there, his eyes meeting Thaddeus' as he said, "What my daddy don't know won't hurt neither of us. And you say men ain't s'posed to be doin' this, but I think you kinda like it, Thaddeus." Pointing down at the towel wrapped around the black man's waist, it was evident that Joey's actions had gotten an obvious reaction.

Looking down at himself, Thaddeus half-frowned and replied, "That don't mean nothin', boy. I just ain't had me a good woman in a long time." He put his dark hands across the front of the tented towel as he said, "Now, you git on back to the big house, Mister Joe. I'm just gonna forgit any of this happened 'n you need to, too."

More determined than ever, Joey said, "I'm not goin' anywhere, Thaddeus. "And you don't need a good woman when you got a good man right here that wants you and…loves you." A look of shock came over Thaddeus' dark face as Joey let his towel drop to the floor and moved forward, grabbing the black man's towel and pulling it away from his body. Locking his eyes on the man's face,

Joey said, dropping down to his knees, "Ain't nothin' wrong with it if it's done for love."

Before the black man could stop him, the young man grasped his hardening cock and began sucking on the head of it in earnest. Thaddeus gasped deeply as he grabbed at Joey's hand and head, trying to stop him. "Mister Joe! Don't be doin' that! You cain't...we cain't...ah mean..." A stifled, low moan came from the black man's throat as Joey suddenly swallowed all of the long, thick cock, deep throating it and making Thaddeus hold onto his head. Joey worked his tongue and mouth on the man's hard cock for several more minutes, then let go, standing up again.

Thaddeus' eyes had begun to glaze over as he had been moments from blowing his load into the young man's mouth. Breathing hard, he started to say something as Joey kissed him again, then took one of his hands as he led them out of the bathroom, headed toward the man's bed.

Two years later, all of Joey's brothers and sisters had married and moved away to start their own families. His mother had passed away two summers ago from a sudden bout of malaria. His father, grief-stricken, had followed her the next winter. Joey had inherited the estate from them as the oldest son. He had promised his father he would run it just as he and their ancestors had done so and had lived up to his word.

As he lay in bed in the large master bedroom, the new master of the estate smiled as the door opened to reveal Thaddeus, wearing his new butler's uniform, carrying a tray containing his morning coffee and newspaper. "Good mornin' Mister Joe," said the black man as he closed the door and came over, setting the tray down on a side table, "Did you sleep good, Sir?"

"Like a rock," replied Joey as the paper and coffee were handed to him. Sipping the coffee, he glanced at the headlines then tossed the paper to the foot of the bed. He set the coffee down on the nightstand as his eyes met Thaddeus'. Grinning, Joey said, "Looks like it's gonna be another hot, hard day today, Thad." The black man smiled back as he began undressing and walked toward the bed.

Lovin' Country

As the bus pulled into the terminal, the elderly woman leaned toward the man in the next seat and said, "Davey? Wake up, we're here."

The man stirred in his seat and opened his eyes slowly, the bright morning sun shining through the open windows. Stretching and raising one hand to shield his eyes, he smiled over at the woman and said, "Oh, gosh. Sorry I drifted off like that. It wasn't the company, ma'am."

The old woman smiled back, saying, "It's fine, young man. You looked like you needed your rest so I just let you."

The bus came to a stop and the driver said over his microphone, "Thank you for traveling with Southeast Bus Lines, ladies and gentlemen. Welcome to Nashville, home of country music. I hope you enjoy your stay here."

The other passengers began to collect their belongings and file out of the bus as the old woman said, "Well, I hope everything works out for you, Davey. You've been a very pleasant traveling companion." She shook his hand and then got up, collected her things and started up the aisle to disembark the bus.

Davey Connor stood up, stretching and stifling a yawn as he opened the overhead compartment and pulled down his backpack, then closed the compartment back. He moved up the aisle with the remainder of the passengers and stepped off the bus, going over to the side to claim his suitcase.

As he waited, he smiled to himself. Nashville, Tennessee. He had finally made it. Away from his former life that now seemed a world away. He didn't know what he was going to find here, but he knew deep inside it had to be better that what he'd left behind.

The driver opened the side panels on the bus and began pulling out the bags and suitcases from inside as the passengers began moving forward to claim them. Davey found his immediately and, slinging his backpack over one shoulder, he grabbed the handle of his suitcase and made his way through the small bus terminal and out the front doors, ready to explore his new surroundings and see what life had to offer him.

———

The old Ford truck came down the street and pulled up to the curb, coming to a stop. The man inside got out, putting his battered cowboy hat on his head, then pulled out the pile of clothes from the backseat. Using his elbow to shut the truck door, he went around the vehicle and into the dry cleaners with the clothes.

As he went inside, he saw the stream of people exiting the bus terminal across the street. Just before the door closed behind him, his eye caught a young man coming out with a backpack and suitcase. Grinning to himself, he thought, "Bet he's come here to make his mark on the world of country music."

===============

Davey stepped out onto the street and looked around, taking in the sights and sounds of the city as the people hurried past him, on their way to different destinations. Deciding that first he needed to find someplace to stay for the night and get a good hot shower after that long bus ride, he turned and walked down the street to the corner. He waited for the light to change, then crossed to the other side and began walking and looking around for a cheap motel.

He looked farther down the busy street and saw a couple of them. The weight of his backpack and carrying his suitcase was taking its toll on his back and he knew he'd be glad to get a room to relax in.

His attention on the two motels on the next block, Davey suddenly found himself walking into somebody hard enough that he fell to his back on the sidewalk, his backpack and suitcase hitting the ground beside him as he said, loudly, "OOOOOFFF!!"

The person he'd walked into replied, "What the...? Oh, damn, man, I'm sorry. You OK?" The man standing over Davey leaned down, his hand stuck out to offer him a hand up.

Davey shook his head as he started to look up at the person standing over him, saying, "Y...yeah, I'm OK, I think. I just wasn't looking where I was going, I guess and..." Whatever he was going to say was lost as he realized who the man was. Grabbing onto the offered hand, he got to his feet and stammered out, "Holy crap! You're...you're...do you know who you are?"

The man in the battered cowboy hat cocked a crooked grin at him, replying, "Well, if you mean I'm Billy Watkins, then I'd have to say 'guilty as charged'. At least, that's what it says on my drivers' license."

Davey smiled and said, "Oh man! I don't believe it! My first morning in Nashville and who do I run into but my all-time favorite country music star! You're a...legend, man! You've been my biggest fan like forever...I mean..."

Billy chuckled at that and said, "I know what you meant, man. Nice to run into a fan, though I don't usually mow 'em down like this. You sure you're OK? You took a bad fall there." The taller man picked up the backpack from the ground, handing it to Davey.

Taking the backpack, the younger man replied, "Yeah, I'm OK." Sticking out his hand, he said, "Davey Connor, Mr. Watkins. I just got here from...well...never mind where I came from. I'm here to start over."

Billy shook the man's hand and said, "Starting over, huh? Well, this town's good for that, for sure. Gonna break into the country music scene, huh?"

Breaking the handshake, Davey said, "Nah, I just needed a new place to start over and Nashville seemed like the best place I could think of." Running his hand through his matted, sweaty hair, he said, "Well, I don't want to keep you, Mr. Watkins. I've got to find a place to crash for the night and get cleaned up. Then, tomorrow, I start looking for a job and a place to live." Throwing his backpack over his shoulder, he grabbed his suitcase again and said, "I can't believe I actually met my idol my first day here! Thanks for taking time to talk with me, Mr. Watkins." Waving a hand goodbye, he turned and started down the sidewalk, headed toward the motels.

Billy watched the man walking away and started to go around to the driver's side of his truck. He watched as Davey moved down the sidewalk and suddenly an idea hit him. Climbing in his truck, he started it up and pulled off down the street. As Billy pulled past Davey, he pulled over to the curb. Reaching over, he rolled the passenger window down and said, "Hey, man! Davey!"

Hearing somebody calling him, he turned around to see Billy's face smiling at him from inside the old truck. He looked around then pointed at himself as Billy said, "Yeah, you! Come over here!"

Davey made his way over to the truck and said, "Hi again, Mr. Watkins! What's up?"

Billy replied, "Well, I just got to thinking and you said you needed a place to crash for awhile and clean up, right?" Davey nodded his head as the other man continued, "I'm heading out for the weekend to my cabin and you're welcome to join me. It's nothing much...just a little place I've got that I like to escape from the city to. But, I can offer you a hot shower and a meal. What do you say?"

The young man's mouth fell open at the offer, then he collected himself and said, "I don't want to put you out, Mr. Watkins. I'd just be in your way. That's awful nice of you to offer, but you've got better things to do than pick up strays like me."

The older man replied, "You ain't putting me out, little man. And, I wouldn't mind the company. Now, throw your stuff in the bed of the truck and get in. I won't take 'no' for an answer."

Davey grinned at that and going to the rear of the truck, he threw his backpack and hefted his suitcase into the bed, then came back up to the passenger door and opened it, climbing in with Billy. Closing the door, he said, "Gosh, I appreciate this a lot, Mr. Watkins. I wasn't really looking forward to spending my last few dollars on some cheap motel. I promise I won't be any trouble, though. You just tell me if you want to be alone, OK?"

As he pulled the truck off down the road, Billy said, "Deal, man. Just one thing, though...call me Billy. My father is Mr. Watkins, OK?"

The young man grinned, replying, "Deal, Billy." Looking down at his rumpled clothes, he looked over at the driver as he said, "I just hope the smell don't get to you, Billy. I usually look a whole lot better than this."

The older man chuckled at that and said, "That's OK, little man. We'll get you that hot shower and a good meal and you'll feel a lot better, I promise." He caught Davey looking at him intently and grinned, saying, "So, I guess you want to know everything about me. After all, I'm your biggest fan, right?"

Davey laughed at that and said, "Aw c'mon Billy. That was an honest mistake and you know it. But yeah, I am your biggest fan. I've heard everything you've ever done and seen you on TV and all. I've read all the articles they've written about you, but I know most of that stuff is just hype, right?"

Billy replied with a grin, "Smart man. Well, let's see..." The truck got on the highway as the country star told his life story to his passenger, unsure about why he was opening up like this, but somehow it just felt right.

―――――――――

A couple hours later, Billy exited off the main highway turning down a dirt road, saying, "It gets a little bumpy from here on, Davey. Hang onto your balls!"

The young man grinned at that as the truck bounced and bumped down the dirt road. As they made the last turn and came around a corner, Davey saw the cabin for the first time. His mouth dropped open as the "little place" that Billy had mentioned was anything but. The all-wood A-frame house was at least three levels with a wrap-around deck around the entire second floor.

Turning to the driver, Davey said, "This is what you call a 'little' place? I'd hate to see what you call big, man!"

Chuckling at that, Billy pulled the old truck up close to the house and shut it off. Both men got out and went to the rear of the truck and started unloading what the country music star had brought along with Davey's backpack and suitcase.

Billy grinned as they went in, Davey's loud whistle at the interior as he closed the door behind them. "I'll take that to mean you like it?"

The young man dropped his backpack and suitcase, his eyes wide as he said, "Damn! This place is amazing!"

Smiling, the music star said, "C'mon. Let's get your stuff upstairs in the spare bedroom. Then, I'll give you the grand tour."

Night began to settle over the house as Davey, now cleaned up and feeling much better, finished eating dinner with Billy. "Feeling more like yourself, little man?"

As the two men cleaned up the dishes, Davey said, "Oh hell yeah! I ain't had a good meal like that in a long time, Billy! A legendary music star and a great cook! What more could anyone ask for?"

Billy grinned at that as he said, "How about we relax in the living room for a while? Then, I bet you'd like a good night's sleep?"

The young man followed his idol as he said, "I could use that, for sure. Though, I don't think I've ever felt more awake than I do right now!"

The two men settled onto the large sofa facing the stone fireplace talking, both somehow knowing that they needed and wanted to get to know one another better. Finally, Billy said, "I guess if we're going to be friends, little man, I ought to tell you everything there is to know about me."

Davey said, "I hope we're friends, man, but what more could you tell that I don't already know?"

The star half-grinned and said, "Well, there are some things that not everybody knows about me." As the young man watched him, Billy took a deep breath and said, "Like the fact that I'm not as straight as the hype would have you believe."

The young man's mouth dropped open at that with surprise, then a grin slowly spread across his face as he replied, "I always wondered about that, Billy. And, by the way, neither am I...straight that is. I always fantasized about that, but that's all I ever thought it was...just a fantasy."

This time it was Billy's mouth that dropped open, then he recovered and said, "Oh man! Now, it's my turn to be surprised! Seems the two of us have more in common that we think, huh, little man?"

Not taking a moment to think, Davey got up off the sofa and took one of Billy's hands and said, "Well, there's one way to take care of that, I'd say." The music star grinned as he stood up and followed his friend upstairs.

━━━━━━━━

Five years later, as they stood before the huge crowd at the yearly awards show, Connor and Watkins looked at each other then at the crowd as they were about to be presented with the "Country Music Duo Of The Year" award.

As the announcement was made, Billy looked at his partner and whispered, "If they all only knew. Nothin' like lovin' country, little man."

Over Your Shoulder

Even after the hurricane that had destroyed his home and all of his belongings, Adam looked on the bright side by telling himself that maybe it was a signal that he needed a fresh start in life and what had happened was meant to be. At least, everyone who knew him got that impression.

In truth, he had no idea of how to start again nor where to start. He had been taken in by friends after the tragedy and he definitely appreciated everything they had done, but after two weeks of trying to come to terms with what had happened, he knew that he had to pick himself up and get his life back on track again.

He decided that if he was going to make a fresh start that he would go all the way...a new town, a new job and a new home. After thanking everyone who had been there for him, Adam explained his plans and was soon ready to begin anew.

He boarded the plane having already checked his luggage in that contained the few things, mostly clothing and personal items, that still belonged to him. He strapped himself in and sat back waiting for the plane to leave.

He had just pulled out a book to read when a man came up the aisle and sat down in the seat next to his. The new passenger smiled at him and said, "Hello. I hope this flight will be a smooth one."

Adam replied, "Hi. Yeah, me too. I've had enough excitement in my life the past few months. I could use a little peace and quiet myself."

The man seated beside him said, "Let me guess. The hurricane, right? You lost everything and you're leaving to make a fresh start?"

"You must be psychic or telepathic. Is it that obvious?" asked Adam.

"Neither of those, but you just look like a lot of people I've seen around here lately," replied the passenger. Extending his hand out, he said, "By the way, I'm Aaron."

Clasping the man's hand, Adam said, "Good to meet you, Aaron, I'm Adam."

Aaron smiled as they broke the handshake and said, "Well, I won't disturb you anymore." Indicating the book in Adam's hands, he said, "I'll let you get back to your reading."

Looking down at the book he was holding, Adam replied, "Not at all. To be honest, it'd be nice to have somebody to talk to. I never have liked plane travel and I only brought this to take my mind off of it."

Smiling again, Aaron said, "That's something we have in common then. I don't care for planes, either. I'd rather travel by other means."

Adam smiled back and said, "I know what you mean. I like going places, but I like to be in the one 'behind the wheel' when I do, if you know what I mean."

Just then, the captain's voice came over the intercom, with his pre-flight instructions. The cabin personnel came through, making sure all the passengers were strapped in and ready.

Aaron looked up and down the aisle and grinned, saying, "Well, too late to back out now, I guess. Here we all go, off to meet our fates."

Adam chuckled at that as the plane began to taxi out to the runway. Several minutes later, they were airborne and leveling off as the plane rose above the clouds.

After the cabin personnel had come through to announce that everyone could remove their seat belts, Adam said, "So, where are you headed to, Aaron? Business or pleasure?"

The man beside him grinned as he said, "Well, that all depends on where I end up, I guess you could say."

Looking puzzled for a moment, Adam asked, "You don't know where you're going? Why would you get on a plane and not know your destination?" Thinking for a moment, he said, "Oh, I get it. You either work for the airline or you're one of those rich guys that just hops a jet anytime he wants, right?"

Aaron grinned and replied, "Well, at least I know you aren't psychic or telepathic. You're wrong on both counts."

Adam asked, "OK, so...how come you got on a plane without knowing where you're going?"

"Well, you see, I travel around a great deal, going from place to place, meeting new people, helping them when I can and so on," replied Aaron.

"So," said Adam, "you're sort of a migratory traveler, then? With the cost of everything these days, I don't see how you can afford to do that."

Aaron replied, "I manage...odd jobs here and there. I live mostly by my wits...with a little help." Leaning back in his seat, the man said, "Well, I think I'm going to take a little nap now, if you don't mind."

"No, not at all," replied Adam.

In what seemed to be a moment, the man beside him was fast asleep, his chest rising and falling steadily as Adam looked out of the window, still thinking about their conversation. Who was this man, who seemed to have no place in mind to be or to live? He didn't seem to let that bother him and gave the impression that he actually enjoyed what he claimed to do.

But yet, there was something more to the man than he was letting on. Adam could not put his finger on it, but deep down inside, he had an overwhelming feeling that there was more to their meeting than just coincidence.

Deciding that a short nap would do him good, Adam lay back in his seat and closed his eyes, his mind still replaying their conversation over and over.

———————

A feeling of warmth with what felt like an electric shock went through him as he suddenly opened his eyes and began to look around. Adam let out a gasp of surprise as he realized he was no longer inside the plane. His eyes widening, he found himself staring into brilliantly-white clouds that were made even more so by the almost-blinding light coming from behind them.

Looking down, Adam almost expected to find that he was standing in mid-air, but quickly realized that his feet were firmly planted on a very solid ground. It came to him suddenly that he was also breathing air in and out as his mind struggled to understand where he was and why he was there.

He moved around in the large brightly-lit area but saw nothing but more of the same clouds encircling him. Finding his voice at last, he called out, "Hello? Is anybody there? Where am I?"

An all-too familiar voice made him turn around quickly as it said, "Hello, Adam. Yes, there are many others here. You're...well, in your frame of reference, you might call this...heaven."

Adam breathed in the air, certain that he was either hallucinating or worse, but managed to say, "Aaron? Is that you? What do you mean I'm in heaven? Did the plane crash? Did we all die?"

As he stood there, Aaron came walking out from one of the nearby clouds, dressed in all-white with a calm look on his face and a smile on his lips. He came up to Adam and said, taking the man's hands in his, "No, the plane didn't crash and no, we aren't dead... well, at least, you aren't dead, but then, neither am I."

Adam struggled to make sense of what Aaron had just said, but was just as confused as ever. "You just said we aren't dead but then..."

Letting go of the man's hands, Aaron placed a finger against Adam's lips and said, "Don't try to understand any of this right now, my friend. Just listen to what I have to say, alright?"

Adam nodded his head in response as Aaron took a few steps back from him. Suddenly, a golden light shone all around the man, making Adam gasp again in a mixture of shock and wonder. Still smiling, Aaron said, "You aren't dead, my friend and you aren't hallucinating, either. I'm an angel, Adam. To be more precise, I'm a guardian angel. Where we are is what we refer to as a midpoint between the hereafter and the earth. Do you understand so far?"

Standing there, Adam nodded his head slowly, but still not understanding everything. Aaron realized this as he continued, "I've been sent to you to let you know that you are making the right choice. You've been under my watch for as long as you've been on the earth, my friend." Moving around in a circle and waiting for Adam to turn with him, Aaron went on. "Haven't you always felt that there was something you couldn't put your finger on? Something that told you that nothing bad could really affect you no matter what situation you were in?"

Adam slowly nodded his head and said, "I...guess so. I've been in bad situations before, but, always somehow, they've worked out for the best. I just put it down to luck. That's what it is, isn't it?"

Shaking his head, Aaron said, "No, the reason you've always come out of those bad situations is that I was nearby to help guide you through them and see that no harm came to you, my friend."

"Wait a minute," interrupted Aaron, "you said you're a guardian angel. Does that mean you're...my...guardian angel?"

Aaron smiled widely at that and replied, "Very good, Adam. And yes, I am your guardian angel. I have been since you were born." Not waiting for his charge to speak again, Aaron said, "It was no accident that I happened to be on the same plane with you. It was necessary for me to take human form and meet you in person. There is something that you and I must discuss and I felt that the best way to do that was to bring you here while you are asleep back on the plane."

Adam said, puzzled, "You mean I'm still asleep and alive on the plane, but I'm here also? So, that means that my soul is here and my body is back...there?"

Aaron nodded and replied, "In a manner of speaking, yes. There's more to it than just that, but for now, that explanation will suffice." He came toward Adam and placed one arm around his shoulders and said, "What we must discuss is of great importance, my friend, and for once, it's up to you to make the choice. This is something I can't help you with this time."

Breathing in the sweet, clean air surrounding them, Adam asked, "What is it that I have to do, Aaron? I can't imagine anything that I could do that would be better than what you could do."

Smiling again as they moved around the cloud-enclosed area, Aaron said, "Simply put, this is what you must decide. As your guardian angel, I'm at the point of my 'life' where I must either leave you and return to non-existence or I can remain the way you see me but in human form. I would become human and mortal from that point on and I would no longer be your guardian angel, looking over your shoulder and protecting you."

Adam replied, "What you're saying is that I have to make the decision to either let you go forever or want you to be real enough and live out a normal life as a human?"

"That's correct, my friend," said Aaron, "and you must make your choice now. Remember this, however, you can't change your mind once you've made your choice. Once the choice is made, it can't be undone, so think carefully."

With that, Aaron removed his arm from Adam's shoulders and moved away back toward the cloud he had appeared from. As he disappeared, his charge heard him say, "The choice is yours, my friend. The choice is yours..."

Adam stood there, transfixed, at what had happened and at the choice he was being offered. His mind raced as he struggled to understand all of this and come to the right decision. He'd never in his life felt so helpless and so unsure of himself as he did just then.

He moved back and forth inside the cloud enclosure as he thought hard about the choice he had to make. He could either lose his guardian angel forever or have him there in real life as a mortal man. Adam looked up above him as if praying or asking for help, when he realized what his decision had to be.

The lights and the clouds seemed to getting brighter as he looked upward and suddenly, he felt himself back on the plane, waking up. He could hear the roar of the engines and the sounds of the other passengers as he struggled to comprehend what had happened to him. Nobody would ever believe him if he tried to explain it.

A thought came to him and he started to open his eyes, but was hesitant and afraid to do so. He whispered, "Aaron? I wish you were still here...with me."

His eyes flew open at the hand that covered his as he turned his head sharply to his left as the man said, "I am here, Adam. You made your choice and now I'm here and always will be here, looking over your shoulder and standing beside you forever."

Forever Yours

"And the winner of this year's Mr. Empire award goes to..." the announcer paused for effect then finished with, "Ray Norton!" as the assembled crowd burst into applause and cheers as the object of their attention raised his arms up in appreciation. The announcer came forward and presented the muscleman with the trophy as the other contestants milled around him to congratulate him on a well-earned victory.

The last of Ray's peers finished wishing him well as the crowd began to disperse and the muscleman felt the wonderful rush of victory at winning this award that he had worked so hard the last year toward achieving. The chairman of the event came up and shook the man's hand, telling him how much he deserved it as Ray glanced out toward the milling crowd.

The chairman's voice suddenly melted into the background as the muscleman found himself staring at one of the audience members who was staring right back at him. It felt as if time had stood still just then as Ray couldn't break his gaze away from the young man standing toward the rear of the auditorium.

Just then, he heard the chairman say, "Well, congratulations again, Ray. You definitely deserved this and I hope you'll be back again next year, too."

The muscleman forced himself to turn away from the man staring at him, saying, "Thank you so much. And you bet I'll be back to defend it!"

The chairman moved off as Ray turned back to look for the young man, but he had seemingly disappeared from the auditorium.

Trophy in hand, the muscleman walked off stage and headed toward the changing rooms and then to the mandatory personal appearance and autograph sessions that he was expected to attend.

Hours later, Ray returned to his hotel suite, tired but happy and feeling on top of the world. Sliding his room key card in the door, he entered his suite and closed the door behind him. Setting the trophy down on a table, he walked over to the sliding doors and went out to the terrace overlooking the downtown area. Stretching his muscular arms out and over his head, he once again thought of the young man in the auditorium and felt a familiar tugging below his waist. Smiling to himself, he said, "Down boy!" then went back into the suite to get himself some juice followed by a hot shower and then a good night's sleep as well.

The muscleman had just finished his shower and was wrapping a towel around his waist when there was a knock on the door. Fastening the towel closed, he came out of the bathroom and went to answer it. Turning the knob and pulling it open, he asked, "Yes? What is it?"

The bellman smiled and said, "This package was left for you at the front desk a few minutes ago, Mr. Norton." He handed the small wrapped box to the muscleman and said, "By the way, congratulations on your win today."

Ray smiled as he took the box and replied, "Thanks. Who is this from, by the way?"

"I don't know, sir," said the bellman, "The manager said the package was at the front desk and nobody saw who left it. I guess you have an anonymous admirer."

Grinning at that, the muscleman said, "I see. Well, thanks again, man." The bellman nodded and left as Ray moved back into his suite and closed the door. "An anonymous package from an admirer," he said to himself, then chuckled as he said, "I don't hear it ticking, so I'm guessing it's not a bomb."

He moved over toward the desk near the front door, sat the package down and began to unwrap and open it. A wide grin came over his face as he pulled out the contents. Inside was a new pair of leopard print posing trunks and an envelope. On the envelope was written "To Ray Norton" and was signed "From Your Future".

Ray pondered the meaning of that as he opened the envelope and pulled out the small card inside that read "We've never met, Mr. Norton, but I'd admired you from afar for a very long time and I just wanted to show my appreciation by sending you this small token which I'm sure you'll not only put to good use but fill out nicely as well."

The muscleman chuckled at that as he sat the card down and held the new trunks up, admiring them. "Well," he said to himself, "I guess it is nice to have fans and I love the trunks. Wonder why whoever sent them wants to remain anonymous?"

Dropping the towel wrapped around his bare body, Ray stepped into and pulled on the new trunks, finding them to be a perfect fit and complimented his muscular body almost like a second skin. Feeling himself get erect again, he moved toward the large mirror on one wall and struck a few poses. "Kind of reminds me of what Tarzan would look like...if he looked like me, that is," Ray said as his hands came down automatically to his encased manhood. He'd abstained from any sexual activity for months now in preparation for this contest, but now he saw no reason to keep himself from pleasuring himself as he turned the lights off and moved over toward the large bed and laid down, his hands squeezing and rubbing over his ever-swelling trunk-covered manhood.

He suddenly felt as though his entire body was floating in air as he worked his bulge when suddenly he realized that he wasn't alone on the bed as two hands followed by a man's body joined him. Wanting to react, Ray found that he couldn't utter a word as the hands moved his aside and began squeezing and groping his bulging trunks. The muscleman's eyes were just adjusting the darkness when he heard a voice say, "Let me bring you the pleasure you need, Ray. You've worked hard to get where you are and now it's time to meet your future."

At those words, the muscleman sucked in air, realizing that whoever this was had to be the same person who had sent the anonymous package to him. He struggled to look down to see who this mystery man was and gasped again more loudly as his eyes met those of the young man's he'd seen earlier in the day.

The man's hands continued to squeeze and massage his bulging trunks as Ray managed to gasp out, "It's...you...from the... auditorium. You sent..."

The man interrupted, saying, "Yes, it's me, Ray." The muscleman started to say something more as the mystery man placed two fingers over his mouth and said, "No more questions for now. Just lay back and relax and let me take over. I promise you won't regret it."

Not knowing why, Ray followed the man's instructions and laid back, closing his eyes as his mysterious admirer slowly peeled the trunks down his legs and went to work on him, bringing the muscular man to the brink of orgasm time and time again, always stopping just before the point of no return.

For what seemed like hours to Ray, the man worked his body sexually like it had never been worked in his life. At some point, Ray had opened his eyes and realized that his admirer was also naked and very muscularly-built as well, reminding him of a smaller version of himself. Several times he wondered if he was only dreaming what was happening, but the sensations he was experiencing were too real to be a dream.

As the mysterious admirer began bringing the muscleman toward orgasm yet again, Ray heard the man ask, "Are you ready to let it go now or do you want me to continue?"

The muscular could smell and feel the sweat that was pouring off both their bodies as he struggled to keep himself from crying out, then said in short, ragged breaths, "Yes...I'm...ready...oh...god...I'm... so...ready...please...I need...to..."

His words were cut off as the man expertly worked his throbbing manhood until, at last, Ray cried out in pleasure, his body twitching and flinching, as he released the pent-up manseed that he'd kept held back for all those months. His brain felt as though it would explode at the incredible sensations going through his body. Lights flashing all around him...his muscles throbbing and vibrating...his manhood expelling all of the pent-up sexual need that he'd denied himself.

Finally, Ray began to breathe more normally as he looked down to see his mystery man cleaning the thick puddles of spent juice that had splattered over his chiseled chest and stomach. A wide grin on his face, the muscleman asked, "I hope now you'll tell me who you are."

The mysterious man replied, "Only that my name is Todd and I've been waiting for a chance like this ever since the first time I saw you. The rest can wait until morning. Now, it's time for a good night's sleep, my handsome god."

Before Ray could say anything, he felt himself being pulled into the smaller man's nude body and held tightly. As he drifted off to sleep, the muscular man murmured, "Please don't be a dream, Todd. Please be here in the morning."

As he dropped off, the man replied, "I'll be here...with you... and for you...yours forever."

A Meeting Of Minds

As John Fletcher drove out through the security gates of Langley Air Force Base, he nodded at the guard and began to relax after what had been a long day at work. As the section head in charge of the biochemical research team, he had grown used to working long hours. However, there were times when he longed for a more peaceful lifestyle and chuckled to himself as he said out loud, "Only fifteen more years and you can retire, John."

He drove his SUV down Highway 64 toward Richmond as he listened to the news on the radio, not thinking about anything else except getting home and a long, hot soak in his tub and a much-needed eight full hours of sleep.

His mind focused on being home, suddenly he was startled as something in the sky caught his attention. It seemed to be a shooting star streaking across the horizon when John realized that it was coming toward him at an incredible speed. Pulling his vehicle over and stopping quickly, he got out and stood there as he watched whatever it was arc across the sky over him, glowing with an intensity so bright that John had to shield his eyes even with the darkness everywhere else.

The object began coming down fast and somehow the scientist knew that whatever it was wasn't going to make a soft landing. He didn't have long to wait as the unknown object suddenly slammed to the ground nearly a half mile away. The force of the impact reverberated through the air, nearly knocking John to the pavement. Grabbing onto the door of his vehicle, he shook his head in amazement as he scanned the area in front of him. Where there should have been at least flame and smoke, he saw nothing. Assuming that the object's impact had sent it below ground level, he started away from his vehicle when suddenly he heard the wailing sirens in the distance. He knew from experience that Langley had dispatched their security teams and had probably been watching the object as well.

Getting back in his vehicle, he started it up and drove on toward home, knowing that tomorrow the base would be buzzing with talk over whatever the object was.

===================

Arriving at the base early after a good night's rest, John was in his office going through some research documents when a security officer called him to meet with the base commander. As he made his way up to the second floor command offices, the scientist had a gnawing feeling that he already knew what the commander wanted.

He entered the office and listened as the base commander explained that an unidentified object had landed outside Langley the previous evening and had been retrieved and brought onto the base for examination. As John listened to what the man was saying, he thought about what he'd witnessed last night, but gave no evidence that he had any knowledge about it.

"The reason I called you in is this, Fletcher," the commander said, "Whatever this thing is, our guys are telling me that it's not one of ours or anybody else's, for that matter."

John sat up as he asked, "It's...alien?"

The man responded, "Yes, Fletcher. Initial examinations are pointing to the fact that we could positively have retrieved a craft from another world." Not waiting for the scientist to respond, he went on, "And...it wasn't unmanned. We found...a being inside."

The scientist said, "A being? You mean, an extraterrestrial?" The man nodded as John said, "Alive or dead?"

The commander answered, "This is top level security, Fletcher. This cannot go any farther than this base, but...yes...whoever this being is, he's alive."

Excitement started to build inside him as John said, "Him? You've already determined gender? Is he able to speak? I mean... communicate with us?"

The uniformed man picked up a folder and opened it, replying, "From the reports that I received this morning, the being resembles a human male, approximately 35-40 years of age." Closing the folder, he looked at John and said, "When he was removed from what we assume was a spacecraft of some type, he appeared to have died. However, when they got him to medical isolation, the doctors examining him suddenly detected a heartbeat and biochemical reactions. He was mangled badly from the crash, but within an hour of being brought here, all of his wounds had healed on their own."

John sat there, processing this information for a moment, then said, "I see. So, you want my team and I to examine the alien and determine how that's possible and attempt to communicate with him. I'm assuming, of course, that no one has tried to talk with him, yet."

Nodding his head, the commander replied, "Actually, the doctors that attended him tried to communicate with him, but even though he was alive and awake, he made no response to them. He also didn't try to resist their treatment. He just laid there, his eyes open but not looking at anyone. They said it was as if he were waiting for something...or someone."

John stood up with the commander and said, "Well, we'll give it our best shot, Sir. I'll try and find out everything I can and have a report of our results to you by this afternoon."

As the commander escorted him to the door, he said, "One thing, Fletcher. I only want you to examine him. So far, only a handful of personnel know of his existence. Because of the seriousness of this matter, the less people that know about it, the better. We don't want this kind of thing being leaked to the outside, even by accident. Do I make myself clear?"

The scientist nodded, saying, "Understood, Sir. I'll report back as soon as I find out anything."

━━━━━━━━━

As he exited the elevator that deposited him underground, John headed toward the medical isolation section, already replaying what the commander had told him in his mind, excited and wondering about who this alien was, where he had come from and what he would find.

He placed his eye at the retinal scan unit at the outside door, which confirmed his identity. The thick steel doors opened, allowing him to enter. As John moved into the room, he suddenly saw the alien laying on the diagnosis bed, sensors and monitors taped to him everywhere. As he came forward, the alien turned his head toward John, this dark eyes meeting the scientist's.

Fixing a smile on his face, the scientist came forward and said, "Hello. My name is Dr. John Fletcher. If you can understand my language, I'm a biochemical research scientist and I've been sent here to examine you and try to communicate with you."

The alien only watched the scientist with his dark eyes as John moved around the diagnostic bed looking at the readouts and displays which showed that the alien, for all intents and purposes, had the same internal structure as a normal human male.

Reading through the printouts and reports left by the medical team, John looked at the alien and said, "Well, you appear to be biologically identical in every way to a male being of our species." He came over to the side of the bed, those dark eyes looking at him. "I wish there were some way for us to communicate, my mysterious friend. I'm assuming that our languages are not compatible, however, if we could somehow communicate, it would help us to understand one another better."

Turning away from the bed to examine another terminal, John began taking notes down in the reports. Suddenly, a voice said, "Under...stand? Lang...uage? H...elp?"

Whirling around, the scientist's eyes went wide as he said, moving back to the bed, "Yes...language...a form of...communication on our world. It helps us to...understand...one another and...help one another."

The alien replied, "This...language you speak of...it is... simplistic...basic."

John smiled again as he asked, "Yes, at times it can be that. Do you understand its basic concepts?"

The dark eyed visitor replied, "Yes...I believe so. The... people...of your world...they do not...communicate...using the same...language. That is...unfortunate."

"Agreed. We don't all speak the same language and that causes many problems between the people of my world. However, we work to understand one another and come to a mutual understanding as best we can."

Suddenly, the alien began to move as he tried to sit up, saying, "John Fletcher. That is...how you are...referred to?"

John raised the head of the bed up to an angle as he replied, "Yes, that is my...name. It is what I'm called. Every person on our world has their own name, if that makes sense to you. Do you have a name or some kind of similar reference that you are called?"

The alien appeared to consider this, then responded, "On my planet, we do not have such references. We are simply...in your language...inhabitants of our world. However, if you wish, you may refer to me as...Cairon."

Smiling at the alien, John said, "Well, it's a pleasure to meet you, Cairon." Reaching down, he clasped his right hand into the alien's right hand and explained, "It's a custom on my world that when people...beings...meet for the first time, they shake hands as a greeting."

Cairon looked down at the hand clasping his and clasped back, squeezing the scientist's hand. "And this...touching...of our... hands...is something that all of your kind practice?"

John smiled again as he said, "For the most part, yes."

The alien narrowed his dark eyes at the scientist as they broke the handshake and asked, "What is that that you do with your face? Your...mouth and the sides of your...face raise up. Is there a meaning to that as well?"

The scientist explained, "Yes, it's called a smile...another form of greeting. It means that the person doing it is pleased to see someone."

Cairon thought that over for a moment, then his mouth and face imitated John's smile, bringing his hand up and feeling the actions of that. "Most unusual, John Fletcher. My fellow creatures have a different way of...greeting...one another. Although, we do not greet one another often as all Caironians are in contact with one another all of the time."

John said, "Planet-wide telepathic abilities?" A confused look came over Cairon's face as the scientist said, "The ability to connect to another being's mind and read their thoughts."

Understanding now, the alien replied, "Yes, we all have that ability. We are born with it and it is as familiar to us as...motion and action."

The biochemical scientist smiled again, saying, "A most interesting concept. The people of our world don't, for the most part, have that ability and those that do, I'm sure they don't have the level of telepathy that you are born with."

Cairon's mouth turned down into a frown as he said, "We find it to be a more open and...honest...form of...communication." As if he were thinking, the alien said, "If you would permit me, I have the ability to connect your mind to mine. It would perhaps...help...both of us to...understand each other."

John raised an eyebrow at that as he said, "I'm not sure that would be a good idea, Cairon. I don't believe you'd find much of interest in my mind, given your superior abilities. But it is..."

Whatever he was about to say John didn't know as suddenly Cairon's eyes met his and the scientist felt as though his mind was falling into a dark hole. Suddenly, there was light again and he found himself still in the room, but something was different. He was seeing images and hearing sounds that he'd never seen or heard before. It was if he were watching a movie of some sort, but was actually there inside the movie.

His brain began processing what was happening and, before he knew it, he realized that what he was experiencing were Cairon's thoughts and memories and somehow knew that the alien was doing the same with his.

Just then, he heard the man's voice inside his head say, "This is the way that my people communicate, John Fletcher. I...apologize for connecting with you, but I felt that it was necessary for you and I to better...understand one another."

John heard his own voice replying back inside his brain, "I understand, Cairon. It was just the initial shock and fear of it that startled me." Looking at one another without saying anything vocally, the scientist said, "The images that I'm seeing and experiencing. They are from your world, I'm guessing. Just as you are seeing and experiencing my thoughts and memories."

The alien smiled again, finding it easier this time as he replied, "Correct, John Fletcher. One thing, however, puzzles me. This...preoccupation, if that is the correct word, that your people have with...what is your term?...sexuality...it is very confusing."

John swallowed hard as he said, "I'm not sure exactly what you're referring to, Cairon. Yes, my people can be very motivated by sexuality between each other, but there are different levels and ideas about that among all of us."

As the alien spoke into his mind again, the scientist somehow already knew what the visitor was referring to. "I apologize for the general reference, John Fletcher. The specific aspect that I refer to is the attraction between two males of your people as well as between two of your...females. I believe your terms for it are...homosexuality and...lesbianism?"

The scientist shifted his feet uneasily as he replied back, "Yes, those are two aspects of our sexuality. There are those among us who are attracted to their own gender rather than of the opposite gender, which we call, heterosexuality."

Not responding for a few moments, Cairon smiled again and said, "I understand now. And, the people of your world that are... homosexual and lesbian...find this to be as normal for them as do the heterosexuals?"

John replied, "Yes. Each person of our world is original and different and we all take different paths based, in part, on our sexuality."

The alien nodded his head as he spoke again, saying, "I find that to be very...interesting. Especially as I'm understanding that you, John Fletcher, are homosexual, are you not?" Receiving what amounted to a gasp from the scientist, Cairon said, "Do not be afraid, John Fletcher. I am simply relating the facts of your mind as you are sending them out. I perceive that your sexuality is not what you would refer to as a generally known fact about you among your kind."

The scientist replied, "That's true, Cairon. On our planet and in this time, there are many prejudices among people in which our sexualities are not acceptable to some. They feel that people like me are not what they would consider to be normal."

Cairon tilted his head as he said, "This...normal you refer to. I assume that it refers to an action or inclination that is not a general preference. Is that what you mean by it not being...acceptable?"

"Yes," replied the scientist.

The alien said, "I see. I feel that your mind is tiring from our contact, John Fletcher. I will break it now and return to communicating with you using our vocal auditory abilities."

The light disappeared again and suddenly the scientist grabbed onto the side of the bed as he heard the alien say, "Are you unharmed? I am now understanding that my method of communication can be...disconcerting to those of your kind."

Taking a deep breath, John said, "I'm OK, Cairon. It's just a new experience for me." Smiling at the alien, he said, "But, not an unpleasant one at all."

The alien's dark eyes looked at him as he said, "I am pleased, John Fletcher. However, this difference in sexuality between your people seems to be based on fear and suspicion. On my planet, we do have such responses. All of my people are free to experience one another in any way that is mutually compatible and agreed upon."

John said, smiling, "It sounds like a utopia to me, Cairon." Seeing the confusion at the use of the word, he explained, "Utopia... to me, it means a society which exists and survives without fear or suspicion and accepts every member on an equal basis and doesn't judge anyone for who or what they are."

Cairon nodded as he said, "I understand now, however, if I am understanding your language, the true meaning of the word is a place not in existence but a goal, perhaps impossible, to strive for."

The scientist nodded his head, saying, "Yes, you are right. I know that our language can be very confusing. Many of our words have more than one meaning."

Looking around the room, the alien asked, "Is it permitted among your people to place your bodies into a nonmoving state for a period of time? I believe you call it...sleep?"

The scientist smiled again as he said, "Of course. I know that this is all very strange and new to you. Please rest now. I have to prepare a report to present to the commanding officer of the base, although, I'm not going to report everything that's happened here. It would..."

The alien interrupted with a smile as he said, "...would cause fear and suspicion about me."

John said, "Yes, most definitely. I would like to continue our conversation later if you would be willing, Cairon."

"I would be happy to have that happen, John Fletcher. I find you to be a most interesting being. I will...look forward...to that."

Boys and Men

Life at the Triple D Ranch was a cowboy's dream come true. Every one of the men employed there were paid good wages and fed well. The local talk was that any man that was fortunate enough to get on with the Triple D had a job for life and not one of them there was about to do anything to screw up the good thing they had going.

The owner, Bret Davis, stood at the window of his master bedroom, sipping his coffee as he looked out at the rolling hills and could hear and see the farmhands as they began stirring and getting ready for another workday. Glancing back to the still-sleeping form in the king-size bed, Bret smiled to himself and began to think back to the day that they got to know each other better...a lot better, in fact.

Bret lay stretched out on a bale of freshly cut hay, one leg raised like a lazy tomcat looking for someone to come along and scratch his belly, his heavy, sultry eyes half closed, but seeing everything. A sprig of hay dangled precariously between two full sensuous lips, occasionally revealing sparkling white perfectly formed teeth, radiant in their contrast to the golden skin tone of a summer tan. His tongue toyed with the sprig, pulling it slowly backward and forward in his mouth, gently biting up and down the stem, sometimes pausing to suck the sweet juices from the hay.

A hawk circled slowly and effortlessly in a clear cloudless sky as an occasional breeze sent a nearby windmill spinning. Bret luxuriated with the feel of the breeze cooling the dampness of his sweat covered hairless skin. He could see the hawk and the windmill and the entire farmstead from his perch high in the hayloft of a large weathered barn. He was also conscious of the light sweet smell of the fresh hay, the lingering smell of livestock, the horses and cattle now out in the pasture and of his own sweat, which he noticed smelled salty and somehow indecently good. Enough so that he raised his arm and nuzzled his nose against the nearly hairless armpit ever so often so that he could enjoy the tangy sensuality of his own smell.

Bret's concentration, however, was not on the hawk or the landscape or on the addictive aroma of his fresh sweat. Instead his half closed eyes focused on the half naked form of a deeply tanned muscular farmhand dowsing himself with water from the horse tank located some fifty yards beyond the barn door.

The clear blue eyes of the sun bleached blond boy turned man reflected the rugged, fully developed frame of the older man as he approached with an easy confident gait that bordered on cockiness. The kind a man has when he feels the world is not only in his pocket, but that he can control all its subjects as well.

Both men had worked since dawn. Joining together to hoist the ninety to one-hundred pound bales of sun-cured hay onto the flatbed of a battered, paint-worn truck. Then, they hoisted the bales from the loaded truck over their heads into place high in the loft.

Although both men had been working at the Triple D for two months, he and the boy had immediately felt a comfortable familiarity and the result was an easy work rhythm which quickly resulted in the clearing of the field and the filling of one side of the barn to the rafters. They knew the ranch foreman would be pleased upon his return at the end of the day from a trip to town for tractor parts. The two men had carefully watched the other since their first meeting. Careful, that is, to appear that they were not consciously doing so.

"Hank Wilson's the name," the hired man had said, extending a firm handshake and a bright, broad smile as he fixed his clear, brown eyes on the younger lad who was to be his working partner. In one quick glance, he sized up the hard, lithe frame of the man-boy, pushing eighteen, admired the hard developing muscles and smooth baby-faced skin toasted golden by the sun's rays and observed the neatly trimmed nearly white sun bleached hair. It was the kid's glistening white teeth and broad generous smile, however, bordered by a dimple on each cheek that captivated his attention and created the basis for the development of an immediate rapport.

The boy's small waist, narrow hips and light frame created a protective urge which sent him rushing to the kid's aid when he saw him attempt to lift a bale far too heavy for his weight. For Bret, eager to show himself to be a man capable of keeping up, unleashed energy which even Hank found himself pressed to match.

Working at the fast, unconsciously-competitive "show off" pace, the men were drenched with perspiration before the first load of baled hay was securely placed in the barn. Small beads of sweat formed rivulets when trickled down their backs as they worked unfettered by shirts which had been discarded by the time the first load of hay had been delivered to the barn from the field. The rivulets converged into a river at the base of the spine, dammed temporarily by the waistline of their Levis only to be released as each stooped to lift another bale, allowing a small flood to gush into the ass crack, soaking the waistline and crotch of each, causing the

Levis to continually ride into the ass and cling seductively to each man's very obvious and more than ample manhood.

Several times during each loading and unloading process, the men unconsciously shifted the cheeks of their ass to lift the center seam of their pants out of the valley in which it had uncomfortably lodged. Or they ran a hand deep into their pants lifting their balls and dislodging the seam permitting the air to circulate, evaporating the sweat and thereby cooling the area concealed by the Levis. Again, unconsciously, the fingers that had been used to separate the damp denim from the wet flesh would be automatically lifted to their nostrils where the sensual smell of fresh, salty crotch sweat would be savored a second or two as they repositioned themselves to toss yet another bale of hay into place in the loft.

As the day wore on, Hank became increasingly aware of the well shaped plump mounds of the boy's small, narrow ass as they stretched and strained against the worn, threadbare pants that barely concealed them each time Bret leaped into the loft to straighten a bale that had failed to land square.

Nor was Bret oblivious of the big, bronzed, handsome stranger. He marveled at the bulging arm muscles as large as his legs and wondered if his own would ever reach that size or achieve the definition each revealed as they flexed and unflexed each time a bale was lifted and tossed as easily and lightly as a twenty-five pound sack of flour.

He also shyly visually examined the massive barrel like chest, matted with dark hair, glistening with sweat, the nipples large and protruding, the hair forming a narrow ridge across hard rippling stomach muscles and around the navel only to rejoin and disappear into the tattered Levis suggesting that even more of the luxurious hair lay concealed beneath. Bret had lain awake many nights wondering how any man could be so big and so perfectly proportioned. At the same time he could not help but wonder if the man's cock would be as large and how would his own compare?

But it was not Hank's muscles or chest or the very large bulge in the worn Levis which captivated Bret's attention or created the restless excitement in his loins. Instead, it was the careless, cat like way in which Hank sensually moved, almost as if every part of his body was independent of the other yet in harmonious coordination. A single toss of the farmhand's head not only seemed to clear the thick, rich brown hair from his eyes, but reposition each strand back into place.

Above all, it was Hank's penetrating dark eyes and the suggestive way he held his mouth when he looked at Bret that aroused the unspeakable sensations in Bret he had not before felt. Bright, large eyes, topped with dark full silky eyebrows and lashes, which smiled mischievously, hinted of excitement and seemed to not only penetrate his private thoughts until he found himself blushing with embarrassment, but which both hypnotized and captivated. And the lips... Firm, determined, masculine lips capable of expressing approval or disapproval, mystery or openness, simply from the way they were held. As well as a hint of something forbidden, like a deliciously dirty private joke which can be shared only in a whisper in close proximity in a private moment.

By the time the first load of the morning had been delivered to the barn, both men already engaged in an easy give and take kidding banter had developed between the two which made them feel like old friends. Horse play was a natural extension of the growing familiarity and a necessity for the excess energy of the younger man. The grab ass began with Bret tossing a cow dung bug onto the back of his older peer. Later a cow chip and a small dead stinking snake were used to taunt Hank until he bulldogged the boy and applied a couple of well-placed solid swats to his firm, full ass. The swats were followed by a finger pushed firmly and deeply through a small hole in the ass seam, causing Bret to bolt and break free from the corn hole invasion only to be tackled again and forced to smell the older man's stink finger after which Hank raised the finger to his own nose to see whether it actually retained any shit smell. Satisfied that it did, he shoved the finger down against Bret's nose, forcing him to smell it a moment longer as penitence before releasing him and resuming their work schedule.

Although the grab ass became more frequent, it did not interfere with their work pace. Instead, it offset any boredom with the monotony of the work and made the day fly by much faster for the two men. To a large degree, they resembled two young bull calves butting and teasing each other, one occasionally taking advantage of an unguarded moment to mount the other in their play, only to have the mounted one break free in mock displeasure from the attempted but sometimes partially successful corn hole. It did not matter that one was much larger and stronger and could easily master the other. It was all part of the horse play game in which all young, healthy, masculine farm boys engage of tease and taunt, of chase and tackle, of domination and submission, and of escape and retaliation.

During the course of the day, Bret had progressively teased Hank. The grab ass had also become increasingly rough, although Bret's fleetness of foot normally permitted him to taunt and then stay just out of reach of the farmhand.

"You fuckin' farthead!" Hank would chide, feigning anger having a cow chip flung his way. "If you don't quit this horse shit, I'm going to beat your ass until you can't sit down."

"Fuck you!" Bret would respond in mock disbelief. "You and who else?" Fully aware that he had best stay on his toes or the farmhand would do it.

A short or threatened chase was always followed by good humored laughter and more verbal threats tossed back and forth.

"I'll take your ass down a notch or two later," he promised. He also knew from the boy's continuation that he would be held to his threatened promise.

Only once during the course of the day had he broken his resolve to maintain the business at hand. It happened in the truck on the return to the field for another load of hay. Hank was driving while Bret was attempting to drink from the water jug. A quick touch of the brake had proved irresistible. The ice cold water splashed down the boy's chest draining around and chilling his hot sweat soaked balls. Bret let out a howl and raised himself off the seat in writhing discomfort as Hank doubled over in uncontrollable laughter. The agonizing gut shaking laughter was Hank's undoing, for with his head momentarily helplessly pressed against the steering wheel he exposed not only his back, but several inches of inviting white ass crack, an irresistibly tempting target for retaliation.

In one spontaneously quick action while Hank was contorted and convulsed with laughter, Bret emptied half the contents of the water jug into the pocket created by the flared out top of the Levis and the exposed crevasse of the farmhand's butt. The shock of the cold water as it ran across his butt hole and spread around his balls instantly froze Hank's hearty laughter and brought the truck to a jolting, grinding halt. Reaching across the truck cab, he grabbed for his blond tormentor. But, Bret's reflexes were too quick and he sprang out of the truck with a graceful leap leaving the door swinging behind. Slamming the truck gears up into neutral, Hank slid across the seat as if it were greased and hopped out the door, landing on his feet close on the heels of the fleeing boy.

They raced in a circle around the truck, both laughing as ice dripped and flew from Hank's pants, both knowing the outcome of the race as they ran. With a lunge, Hank tackled the boy, wrapping his massive arms around the boy's waist to drag him to the ground. Panting, still laughing, they collapsed in an exhausted heap, the older, larger man squarely on top of his smaller, younger prey.

"You shit head," Hank laughed. "You're going to suck ass now!"

"Say's who?" Bret mocked, knowing full well the big farmhand could force him to eat prunes out of his asshole if he were of a mind to do so.

For several minutes they lay panting while Hank recovered his breath from the chase and determined an adequate retaliation for his helpless captive. As Bret lay pinned in the soft grass, he found himself becoming increasingly aware of the pleasure of having the weight of the large, handsome man's body pressed tightly against his own. He could even feel the fullness of the farmhand's large dick through the two thin layers of Levi material as it lay across his own. And for a moment, he found himself pushing his own hips up slightly to increase the excitement of the contact until in the process he was alarmed to feel his own cock expand and grow from the pressure.

The pleasure of the contact was increased by the mingling of their body smells. Sweat dripped from Hank's overheated armpits, forehead and chest onto the face and chest of the younger man. Hank's cheek rested on Bret's so that the boy found himself not only being covered with the farmhand's sweat, but forced to breathe his breath as well.

Hank was fully aware of the blond farm boy's cock as it expanded, lengthened and hardened against his own hardening rod and he was tempted to strip the pants from the boy and spend the remainder of the day playing with this new found toy. But the time of day, the work at hand, and the open field shaped his judgment and made him realize that some modified course of action was called for.

Raising himself slightly, he tightly gripped the boy's chin with one large hand and roughly turned Bret's face into his own. "Give?" he both harshly questioned and demanded, his face almost brushing Bret's. "No more horse shit until we get our last load hauled in for the day. Okay?"

Receiving no response, he thrust a hand into the boy's pants, popping the buttons of the Levis, until he held two smooth, hairless balls and an already man-sized cock in his massive grip. Finding the base of the balls and dick with his forefingers, he gave a quick twist which extracted a yell of pain.

"Okay! Okay!" Bret yelled in response, reluctant to loose the contact of Hank's hand on his highly sensitive cock, but not anxious to have his nuts twisted again.

A grin spread across Hank's face. Mischievous and mocking, his breath hot and sweet smelling, continued to blanket his captive's face.

"Open your mouth!" he ordered.

"What?" asked Bret, the puzzlement showing in his eyes.

"Open your mouth, damnit!" Hank ordered as he tightened his grips on both the boy's face and balls.

The mouth opened wide like a baby bird's ready to receive a mouthful of nourishment. And before Bret realized what had happened, he had accepted and swallowed a full mouth of Hank's spit.

"You fuckin' son of a bitch," he muttered, but without conviction. The spit had tasted sweet and he found himself wanting to taste not only more of the spit but all of the man that now dominated him.

Laughing, Hank then pretended he was fucking his young ward and he felt the boy's prick swelling even more and jumping with excitement between his calloused fingers as he moved his hips up and down in the mock rape.

Then, without warning, he raised his crushing weight up off of the boy, and placed his knees across each of the boy's arms so that he was still securely pinned to the ground. A smelly fart ripped from his ass in the process and he laughed knowing the boy's nose would get the full benefit of his earthy expulsion.

Bret struggled unconvincingly for he now found himself excited anew by the nearness and smell of his conqueror's crotch and its hidden tantalizing, but fully obvious massive hard containment.

His nose enjoyed the heavy smell of the fart and of the sweat soaked section of Hank's denims plastered to the skin between the asshole and the base of his extremely large balls which now loomed directly over Bret's face.

Without warning, Hank ripped the front of his tight Levis open and pulled them down to his knees resulting in their serving as a restraint across Bret's neck. Bret's eyes grew large and his mouth fell open in amazement. He could tell from the bulge in those Levis that his working partner had one hell of a pole. But what now dangled only an inch from his nose was the largest prick he had ever seen.

Horse dick is the only comparison of which Bret could think and he wondered how anyone that big could ever fuck anybody without splitting them in two. Bret's own man-sized cock stood straight up like a flag pole as his eyes feasted with excitement on the milk white ass which hovered only a couple of inches above his head and the massive hairy balls, larger than chicken eggs which Hank proceeded to rest on the boy's mouth and chin.

Never had Bret imagined that another man's balls and dick could smell so good although he had often enjoyed the smell of his own sweat from the same two areas. The dick, he noticed, smelled of sperm and he found it the most sexually exciting smell he had ever encountered. His eyes looked almost straight down the tremendous prick in near sighted fashion since the head of the dick was now resting against the end of his nose as Hank reached back and grabbed Bret's own ample endowment causing spasms of pleasure to ripple through the boy's loins and spread throughout every inch of his body.

A drop of clear fluid appeared out of the nearly inch wide opening of Hank's cock, and dripping down onto Bret's lips left a connecting string between the cock and the full succulent lips. The slipperiness of Hank's hand on his own cock made him aware that he was also dripping in the same excited way. Hank used his other hand to grasp his own tool and Bret watched helplessly as the cock began to expand even further until the head fully cleared the skin which had previously covered all but the tip end.

Bret knew that the excitement of Hank's touch and his own still boyish sensitivity would produce an uncontrollable explosion from his innards within seconds. He writhed and twisted in his agonizingly enjoyable predicament and prayed to himself, "Please, please, don't let me shoot first." Almost as if his prayer had been answered, he watched the large veins on the side of that massive cock swell and expand. He swore he could actually see the tremendous rod jump another quarter of an inch larger in length and diameter.

Hank quickly raised himself up off the boy and pushed the monster prong straight back between his legs. Bret watched in a hypnotic totally sexually aroused state as spurt after spurt of thick white pudding shot onto his own spurting cock, his stomach and chest; he in turn, bulls eyed the ass that hung over his head.

Without saying a word, Hank took his sperm-covered hand and rubbed it thoroughly over Bret's chest and stomach and down all over his balls and dick until the expended life cells from both men had been not only completely mixed, but absorbed into the boy's smooth, flawless skin. He then raised himself upright, directly over the boy's face and after squeezing the still massive, but softening prick a couple of times, he began to piss a full yellow stream around Bret's head, never quite touching the boy's hair or face, but causing considerable alarm as Bret apprehensively watched the stream as it appeared to be directed straight for his face.

Finished, Hank deliberately shook the last few drops of piss off of his peter into the boy's face and hair. Then removing his now painful weight from Bret's body, he stood up and nonchalantly pulled up and buttoned his pants.

"That, motherfucker, is just a sample of what you can expect if you fuck around with me," he said, walking back to the truck without a backward glance.

Bret slowly got up. Noticing and smelling the ring of piss-foam and soaked earth that had encircled his head as he did so. Also aware of the tightening feel of his cum soaked drying skin. And without a word, Bret climbed back into the truck with Hank to finish their day's work.

The last load of hay was delivered into place a good two hours ahead of what might have been anticipated. Although the foreman had not expected the two men to clear the field early, he had told them that morning that they could knock off work after the last load had been placed in the barn just in case they should exceed his expectations. He knew that hauling in all the bales in the field was enough work for any two men on a given day.

As Bret watched Hank enter the barn and climb the step ladder leading to the loft where he lay, he was filled not only with the satisfaction of a job well done, but with more excitement and expectation than he had ever known. He remembered absolutely every detail of the early afternoon struggle in the hay field and he was anxious to experience it all again. It was as if something inside of him had been awakened and aroused. And, like a filly in heat, he felt he had not had nearly enough of this tall, dark, handsome man-stallion.

Tired but not worn out, relaxed but ready for a new encounter, he wondered how he might taunt the older man into another rough game of grab ass. Only, this time, he had an idea of just what he might be getting himself into and he looked forward to again being the conquered loser.

===========

Suddenly, the feeling of two hairy, muscular arms snaked their way around Bret's jean-clad waist, bringing him back to reality. Grinning as the feeling of a pair of lips on the back of his neck, Bret twisted around to nothing but thin air. Again, reality hit him as he remembered the accident that had cost Hank his life just three months ago, leaving him the now-sole owner of the Triple D.

Pushing back the tears threatening to well up again in his eyes, Bret went over to one of the large closets and opened it, pulling out one of Hank's favorite denim shirts. Holding it against his nose, the young ranch owner could swear he could still smell the man's musky scent in the material. Putting the shirt back, he went over to the large dresser near the window and picked up the framed photograph of the two of them. Smiling to himself, Bret said, "Hank...damn you..."

A Boner Book

Blue and Grey

Moving through the woods, his bayoneted rifle at the ready, he searched through the thick area for any hidden or wounded men who had tried to escape the battle at Northport. Corporal Anthony P. Adams was a model soldier in his company and had risen through the ranks quickly on his own merits. Obviously, the fact that his great-great-great-grandfather had been John Adams, one of the original authors of the Declaration of Independence had not been a detriment, but Anthony was proud of his accomplishments nonetheless.

He'd joined up with the Northern army just after the Civil War had begun and had seen his share of fighting and killing as had the other men in his company. He was being groomed by his father to join him in his law firm, but when the war started, he put aside his career to fight the rising Southern troops, believing as all Northerners did that they were trying to encroach and take over. Even though he'd been decorated four times for bravery beyond the call of duty, Corp. Adams was not one to let medals and awards deter him from the goals of his company.

As he moved as quietly as possible, he could see the daylight above the trees already starting to disappear as night approached. Keeping his eyes and ears open for any sound that might give away an approaching enemy, he had orders to kill any of them that he found, wounded or not. He could hear the crickets and other night creatures stirring as he scanned the area for anything.

He had been in the woods for nearly two hours and had not seen or heard anything from any man. Deciding to take a short rest, he lowered his rifle and leaned it against a large tree. Pulling his canteen off of his belt, he opened it and took a satisfying drink, enjoying the feeling of the cool water as it flowed down his throat.

That was the last memory he had as the butt of a rifle slammed against the side of his head, knocking the canteen from his hand as he lost consciousness and fell to the ground.

———

The sound of night creatures were the first thing he was aware of as he slowly came to, his eyes opening slightly. His head was throbbing and he could feel the dried blood matted in his long, dark hair as he struggled to remember what had happened and, more importantly, who had attacked him and where he was. His first thought was that he had been captured by the enemy and would soon be either imprisoned or killed.

As his head started to clear, Anthony realized he was sitting on the ground against a large wooden post that had been driven into the ground, his hands tied tightly behind his back. His rifle and ammunition had been taken from him as well as his boots. Testing the ropes that held him, he quickly realized that whoever had captured him had no intention of allowing him to escape. Opening his eyes wider now, the corporal saw that wherever he was, it was only himself and his attacker/captor.

There was a large tent about twenty feet away with a campfire blazing away in front of it. Looking at the tent, he could see someone moving around inside and knew he would be facing his captor very soon. Anthony smelled the food being cooked on the campfire and his stomach rumbled as he remembered that he had not eaten since the previous day. He had heard rumors about these Southerners, that they would starve a man to death as a form of torture before killing them.

He thought about his family back home and tried to imagine what their reaction would be when they got word that he'd been captured and killed. He'd left behind his mother and father as well as the fiancé that'd he become engaged to shortly before he'd enlisted. He'd made a promise to them that he would come back, but now it looked as though he would be unable to keep it. He knew that they were all proud of him, remembering their faces as the train had pulled out of the station, the three of them waving goodbye with tears streaming down his mother's and fiancé's face.

Pushing those thoughts to back of his mind, the corporal tried again to loosen the ropes holding his arms tight, but they held fast. Could he try and reason with his captor and somehow escape? From what he'd heard about Southerners, most of them were uneducated and joined the war because they weren't fit for any other occupation.

As he sat there, trying to come up with some kind of plan of action, the flap of the large tent was pulled aside. A dark figure came out, leaving the flap open and started moving toward the campfire. As the corporal watched, the man continued cooking the food and added a coffeepot onto the grate over the fire. The smells of the food and the coffee assailed Anthony's nose, but he was determined not to give in to it.

The figure picked up a metal plate and cup and filled it with some of the food and coffee and quietly consumed the meal as his captive watched. The man glanced over in Anthony's direction a few times as he sat there eating and drinking, but the corporal couldn't make out anything about the man other than the fact that he was wearing the standard grey uniform of the enemy. His own blue uniform was dirty and sweaty and he could feel it sticking to his body, even through his underclothing.

The man finished his meal and stood up, scraping the plate into the fire. Setting the plate down, he picked up his metal cup and sipped at the coffee as he stared into the fire. Anthony thought he was probably deciding how long he would keep him captive before either turning him over to his superiors or killing him outright.

As he watched, however, the man sat his cup down next to the fire and picked up another plate and cup, filling them. He turned and started toward the captured soldier. The corporal let his head drop, feigning sleep, not wanting the man to know he was awake. He could hear the man's boots moving closer, then felt one of them nudge one of his legs.

Expecting the typical Southern accent from his captive, Anthony was surprised when the man said, "Wake up, corporal. I thought you might want some food and drink. No sense in starving you to death, after all."

The bound man raised his head and looked up into the face of his captor as he said automatically, "Name...Adams, Anthony P., Rank...Corporal...Bravo Company, Commonwealth of Virginia."

The man smiled and replied, "Well, Adams, Anthony P., I'm Jeremiah A. Taylor, also a corporal and from Delta Company out of Savannah, Georgia. Now that we've been introduced, how about some food and drink?"

Almost shaking his head no, Anthony felt his stomach rumbling and his thirst overtaking him as he saw clearly the face of his captor. He sucked in his breath as Corp. Taylor knelt down, placing the plate on the ground and reached behind his prisoner and began untying his bound hands. "Guess it'd be a little easier to eat with your hands, wouldn't it, Corporal?" the man asked. "Just don't think about running off and trying to escape, though. I've got traps set all around the perimeter of the camp and you wouldn't spot them until it was too late."

His hands free at last, Anthony's first impulse was, of course, to attack his captor and attempt an escape, but not knowing where the man had set the traps made him think twice about that. As he rubbed his sore wrists, Jeremiah picked up the plate and cup and pushed them toward him, saying, "Go ahead and eat, it's not poisoned by the way. And, contrary to popular belief, us Southerners don't starve our prisoners."

That last remark brought a slight grin to Anthony's face that was answered by a grin from his captor's. Taking the plate, the corporal said, "Thank you for the food." He began eating at the food and drinking the coffee, thinking it was the best meal he'd had in a long time. The two men's eyes met a few times as he consumed the food and Anthony thought he detected a twinkle in Jeremiah's eyes as the Southern corporal watched him eat.

"So, tell me, Adams, Anthony P.," the man started, "didn't anybody ever tell you not to rest when you're hunting for the enemy? I spotted you a few yards away and had you right in my line of fire when you stopped at that tree. If you'd come any closer, you might be laying there with a bullet in you instead of sitting here eating, you know."

The corporal swallowed the mouthful of food and said, "You saw me coming? How in the hell did you stay covered up? I didn't see anybody around as far as I could see."

Jeremiah remained on his haunches as he smiled and replied, "That's 'cause grey blends in better in the woods than blue, Corporal. That and me laying among a few well-placed branches makes for good camouflage, you know. That blue uniform of yours in these woods stands out like a blue jay just waiting to get caught."

Anthony finished his meal and looked down at his dirty blue uniform, then looked up and said, "I guess you're right about that." Handing the empty plate to his captor, he said, "So, when do we go back to your company so you can turn me in? Provided I don't manage to escape between now and then, that is."

Taking the plate, Jeremiah raised up again and motioned for Anthony to get up and join him by the campfire. Grabbing his cup of coffee, the Northerner followed behind him and sat down on one of the two rocks serving as chairs. "Well," started Jeremiah, "Like I said, you won't escape out of here cause of the traps I set. As far as taking you back and turning you in..."

Anthony swallowed a mouthful of the coffee as he had a sudden thought that he had assumed that his captor was planning to turn him in rather than kill him outright.

Jeremiah saw the flash of fear pass over his captive's eyes as he said, "Don't worry, Corporal. No, I ain't planning on killing you. I wouldn't kill a man unless he gave me a good reason for it." He saw the corporal relax again as he continued, "But, I ain't planning on taking you back and turning you in, either."

His captive smiled and said, "But, you aren't planning on just letting me go, either, right?"

The man seated next to him replied, "You're right about that, Corporal." He poured more coffee into their cups as he said, "See? I'm kinda in a bit of trouble myself." Before Anthony could ask, he continued, "I was sent out by my company just like you only that was more than a month ago. I've been living out here 'cause...I've decided not to go back."

Anthony replied, "Not to go back? You mean you're deserting?"

Jeremiah said, "Call it whatever you want. I just don't see no sense in this damn war. What good is it to live in these supposedly-new United States if every man is fighting against each other? That don't seem like it's real "united" to me."

The Northerner replied, "But, you can't just walk away from your duty and obligation! We've both been ordered to defend our borders and any man that tries to walk away would be shot as a deserter!"

His captor replied, "Duty and obligation? Whoever said that it was a man's duty and obligation to kill his fellow man, sometimes killing his own brother? That doesn't make a damn bit of sense! If this country is gonna survive, we all better wake up fast and realize it's only gonna happen if we all work together instead of against each other!"

Anthony said, "Well, I understand what you're saying, but what are you going to do? How are you going to get away? Where are you going to go?"

Jeremiah replied, "As far as getting away, I'm sure my company probably thinks I'm already dead since I ain't returned back. I figure all I got to do is wait it out a few more weeks and I can just disappear somewhere."

His captive said, "Disappear somewhere? How are you going to do that in that uniform?" A thought occurred to him as he said, "If you're going to just disappear, what do you plan to do with me?"

The man smiled and said, "Well as far as the uniform goes, I've got some civilian clothing that I snuck out here with me, so I can just lose my uniform wherever I need to." Taking another sip of his coffee, Jeremiah said, "And, I was kinda hoping that you might want to come with me. I've got some relatives that are out West that we could stay with. And, I've got enough clothes for both of us."

Anthony looked at the man as though he'd lost his mind. "Me? Just pick up and leave? Desert the army and my family?" Shaking his head, he said, "I couldn't do that to them. I've got a fiancé back home and my parents and a promising law career to look forward to. I agree that this war doesn't make any sense, but what you're suggesting could get us both killed or worse."

Jeremiah finished his coffee and reached up, unbuttoning his grey uniform jacket. Anthony glanced at him as the man's bare, hairy chest came into view. Suddenly, he felt a twinge coming from inside of him, a feeling he'd never had before as his mind raced to comprehend everything that his captor had said.

Pulling the jacket off his body, Jeremiah threw it over toward the tent. Anthony had a full view of the man's lean, hairy body as another twinge shot through him. He hadn't taken the time to really look at the man who'd captured him, but now with the man stripped to the waist, the corporal suddenly found himself lost in the vision as he realized how handsome the man was. His mind was racing with feelings he'd never experienced before and he found his body reacting like it never had before.

He'd heard about other men who had been thrown together for long periods of time without the company of a woman and found ways to satisfy themselves, but he had never considered or even thought about doing that. He'd never found himself attracted to another man before and he struggled to push the thoughts from his mind as he tried to think about his parents and his fiancé.

Jeremiah saw the look on Anthony's face and smiled inwardly as he knew what was going through the corporal's mind. Coming from the South, it wasn't anything out of the ordinary for two men to be together. He'd had a few male lovers in his time and, in fact, had left one back in Savannah when he'd enlisted.

Finishing his coffee, the Southerner set it down and looked at Anthony dead in the face and said, "We could do this, Mr. Adams. Together, we could get out of this insanity before one or both of us get killed. Nothing good will ever come of this war and we both know it. Nobody would ever know what happened to either of us.

All we have to do is agree to do it and stick together and we can make this happen."

Anthony finished his coffee, handed the cup to his captor and said, "This all makes sense...perfect sense, in fact. But, just to pick up and disappear like that? I've just never thought about doing something like that. Frankly, it terrifies me, Jeremiah."

The man seated next to him nodded and said, "You think I'm not afraid to do this? I'm scared shitless, too. But, like I said, the two of us could do this. Safety in numbers and all, you know."

Shaking his head, Anthony unbuttoned the top of his uniform jacket down halfway as he felt the sweat running down inside it from the fire. Jeremiah smiled at that as their eyes met again, saying, "We can do this, man. Together. You and me. A team."

Anthony suddenly realized that Jeremiah had moved closer to him, obviously having the same feelings he was. He put a hand on the man's bare shoulder and said, "But, what if..."

Before he could finish, he suddenly felt Jeremiah's bare arms around him, pulling them together. Anthony started to protest, but discovered his arms around this captor as well. Their mouths came together, both of them grunting deeply as they kissed hard and long, their tongues coming together. Lost in their embrace, both men stood up and their hands began fumbling at each other's clothing in front of the hot fire.

Minutes later, both men, Northerner and Southerner were bareassed and still holding onto each other as they moved away from the fire toward the large tent together.

———————————

A week later, as both men finished breaking the camp down, both dressed in regular clothes, Anthony looked over at his former captor and grinned and winked. Returning the wink, Jeremiah finished covering the hole he'd dug and discarded their uniforms in and said, "That's about it. You ready?"

Anthony finished closing their backpacks and came over, handing one to the other man. "Ready here. You and me, right?"

Jeremiah kissed him again, then slung his backpack over his shoulders and replied, "You and me. We can do anything. Together. Forever."

Needs Of A Friend

Jake walked through the woods with a mixture of happiness and sadness as he neared his destination. He had been coming to the old, abandoned house for many years now, in fact, since he was ten years old. It wasn't that he wasn't happy at home, but after stumbling across the old house, he found that he'd grown attached to it and it was a place he could come to when he needed to be by himself with no one else around.

Now twenty-one, he would be leaving next week for a new job in a new city and knew that he had to pay a final visit to his private domain. As he trudged through the overgrown woods that evening, he thought back to all the times in the past when he'd been struggling with a problem and escaped to the old house to think things through and decide what to do next. The fact that he was not alone when he visited the house was something that he'd always kept to himself. The first few times he had been there he had always felt that someone or something was there as well, but try as he might, he could never find any proof that that was so.

═══════════════

On his fifth visit, however, he was wandering around through the first floor when he heard a voice say, "Jake? If you are in need of a friend, all you need to do is call out. I will be here for you, always." He tried in vain to discover who was there with him, but there was no one there. As he left the house later that night, he turned around and, for a moment, thought he had seen the figure of a young boy about his age at one of the upper windows waving at him, but when he blinked his eyes, whoever it was had vanished. Dismissing it as his young, overactive imagination, he continued on home.

He did not have an opportunity to go back there for a week owing to school work and family matters, so he was looking forward to another visit to his supposedly-private retreat. The next opportunity presented itself the following Friday and Jake, determined to discover if he'd just imagined the voice or not, waited until his parents were asleep and snuck out, making his way as quickly as possible toward the old house. Carrying a sleeping bag and a flashlight, he made his way through the dense woods, exiting into the clearing just before the front door of the old two-story house.

Jake shone the flashlight on the front door when something above caught his eye. Glancing up toward the second-story windows, again he saw what he thought was a figure of that same boy, but when he raised the flashlight up, there was nothing there. He had to be just imagining it, he told himself. Nobody had lived in the house for many years. Jake didn't have any close friends so he knew it couldn't be someone playing a prank on him.

Shrugging it off, he went up to the front door and turned the handle, opening the unlocked door and making his way inside. Closing the door behind himself, he made his way into what was once a large living room and unrolled his sleeping bag on top of an old, dusty sofa in the center of the room. The house was devoid of furniture for the most part, the sofa being one of the few remaining items still in one piece.

As he had done many times before, Jake began exploring the darkened interior with his flashlight, looking around every corner just in case he found something or someone besides himself there. After completing his search, the young boy gave up and went back downstairs to the sofa. Shutting off the flashlight, he climbed into the sleeping bag and soon was fast asleep.

Suddenly, something brushed against his face and Jake woke up quickly, calling out, "Who-who's there?" His eyes adjusted to the darkness now, he looked around him but still couldn't see anything that would have caused it.

Just as he was settling down again, the young boy looked down toward the end of his sleeping bag. Sitting there at the end of the sofa was another young boy, about his age, looking at Jake and smiling at him. At least, whoever it was looked like a young boy. The only difference was that this young boy was transparent and he could see right through him and into the next room.

Sitting up slowly, but shaking some with fear, Jake asked, "Who are you? Where did you come from? Are you a...a...ghost?"

The apparition continued to smile at him as he spoke. "Don't be afraid, Jake. I won't hurt you. I want to be your friend."

Keeping his eyes on whatever it was sitting there, Jake said, "I'm...not afraid. I've just never met a real...ghost before. What's your name?"

The transparent young boy replied, "I'm Joseph. And, yes, I guess I'm what you'd call a ghost."

Jake asked, "What are you doing here, Joseph? I thought this house was deserted and abandoned? Nobody's lived here for a long time."

Joseph smiled again, saying, "Yes I know, Jake. I used to live here when I was...alive. This is my father's house. We lived here nearly a hundred years ago, but then..." His voice trailed off and the smile on his transparent face was replaced with a look of sadness.

Jake sat up more and asked, "But what, Joseph? You look so sad. What happened to your family and to you?"

The young boy replied, "There was an outbreak of malaria that spread quickly through the town and all of us were infected. My parents and brother were the first to go. I was the last one to die."

"But, if you all died here, how come I can't see your parents and brother?" asked Jake.

Joseph said, looking around the darkened room, "They passed over, I guess. I've been waiting to join them all this time, but something kept me from going to where they are. I miss them a lot. I've been so lonely here." Looking back at Jake, the young boy said, with a smile, "And then you started coming here and I didn't feel so alone anymore. I hid for a long time from you because I didn't want to scare you. I used to listen to you talking to yourself about your problems."

Jake smiled now as he said, "Yeah, I like to come here when I need to figure something out and it always seems to help. There's something about this place that makes me feel...oh, I don't know... calm and happy."

The two young boys continued to talk until Jake noticed that the sun was starting to come up in the sky and said, "I've got to leave now, Joseph. The sun is rising and I don't want my parents to know I've been gone all night. Nobody else knows that I come here... except for you, I mean."

Joseph smiled and said, "I understand, Jake." His spectral form rose off the sofa and turned toward his new friend as he said,

"You will come back again, won't you? I like it when you come to visit."

Jake rolled his sleeping bag up and grabbed his flashlight. Turning toward Joseph, he smiled and said, "You bet I'll be back. It's nice to know there's somebody I can talk to like a...friend."

The young ghost smiled again. "Like I said to you the first time, Jake. If you need a friend, I'm always here. All you have to do is call my name."

With that, the spectral form vanished into thin air. Jake looked at the space where Joseph had been for a few more minutes, then quickly left the old house and headed for home before his parents could wake up and find him missing.

$$===============$$

Jake suddenly found himself standing there in front of the old house as he returned to the present and, as always, he turned the flashlight on and flashed it at the front door. That had become the signal that he used to let Joseph know he was there.

As if on cue, the front door opened by itself, allowing Jake to enter and closed behind him. He went into the living room and spread out the sleeping bag on the floor instead of the sofa. Turning the light off, he sat it down on the sofa.

"Welcome back, Jake," said the voice behind him. Turning around, he saw Joseph standing there, with open arms and a smile on his face.

"Thanks, Joe," he replied.

Quickly, he moved forward toward the now grown-up ghost with his arms extended and felt the transparent form enveloping his body as his arms moved around it to hug it back. The two men stood there for a moment then broke the hug and moved together toward the sleeping bag, Jake sitting down on it and Joseph's form settling down on it as well.

Joseph said, "You haven't been here in a long while, my friend. I hoped that nothing had happened to you."

Jake replied, "No, nothing happened to me...well...nothing bad, anyway."

The ghostly form cocked his transparent head to one side and asked, "Something good happened to you?"

Smiling Jake said, "Yeah and that's why I had to come to see you, Joe. I have some news that I don't know how you're going to take."

Joseph brought a transparent hand up to the man's shoulder and said, "What is it, Jake? Please tell me."

A feeling of warmth went through Jake's body as he said, "Well, I've just been offered a new job in a different city and so I'm going to be moving away. I won't be able to come back here for a long time."

The two men's eyes met as the ghost said, "I see." Jake saw the frown coming over the man's transparent face as he said, "I always knew this day would come but I always hoped that it never would."

Jake said, "I know...me too. I don't want to leave, Joe, but I have to. I just wish there were some way for you to come with me. I don't want to leave you behind. You're the best friend I've ever had."

He watched as Joseph's form stood up again and began pacing back and forth across the darkened living room. Finally, the ghostly image stopped and turned toward Jake, saying, "I don't want to be here without you, either, Jake. I want to be with you, forever. I...I... love you, Jake."

The young man smiled at that and replied, "I love you too, Joe. I wish there were a way..."

Interrupting, Joseph said, "You must leave Jake, now. I can't explain it to you right now, but you must go and never come back here again."

Jake's eyes widened as he said, "But, I want to stay...here... with you...one last time, Joe. I..."

Joseph looked into his eyes and said, "No, you have to leave now, Jake. Leave and don't look back. Please...if you truly love me, you'll do this."

Before Jake could respond, the spectral figure disappeared again, leaving him alone in the darkened room. Without realizing it, the young man found himself rolling his sleeping bag up and taking his flashlight. He was halfway through the dark woods before he'd realized that he'd walked out of the abandoned house. Suddenly, a enormous feeling of sadness came over him as he realized that he would never see Joseph again.

He made his way through the woods back toward his parents' house for the last time, his shoulders slumped and a sense of loss flooding his entire body.

═══════════

A year later, Jake had settled into his new life and job in the big city, having been promoted to head of his department recently. He'd only just recently come out to his parents and to people he knew in the city and was surprised to find that they all accepted his news positively and wanted nothing more than for him to be happy.

Still, there was still the gnawing feeling of loss that he carried with him in the aftermath of leaving Joseph and the old house behind. Jake knew he had to move on and put the past behind him, but he still dreamt at night about being with Joseph and the two of them being together forever.

The next morning he went into work and was in his office when a co-worker stopped by to advise him that the new hires were coming in and would be starting today. Jake had been approved for two new people in his department and got up from his desk to go and greet them.

One, a twenty-something attractive woman, would be working in the secretarial pool and Jake greeted her and welcomed her to the company, showing her around the office and introducing her to her new co-workers.

After getting her settled in, he came back to greet the other new hire who would be working as his assistant. He came down the hallway and saw the supervisor of personnel facing him and a young man with his back turned toward him. Coming forward, he greeted the supervisor with a handshake. The supervisor said, "I want you meet your new assistant, Jake." The young man turned around and smiled as Jake blurted out, "Joseph? What the hell? How can you..."

The supervisor had a puzzled look on her face as she said, "This is Joseph Baldwin, Jake. He'll be your new assistant. Have you two met before?"

Joseph turned toward her and said, "No, we haven't met before. But, a lot of people tell me I look like people they knew...in their past."

She nodded and left the two men standing there as Jake took Joseph by one arm and led him down the hall into his office, closing the door behind them. "It IS you, isn't it, Joe? But, how can you be here? Alive and...?"

Joseph smiled and said, as he opened his arms toward Jake, "I told you I didn't want to be without you, Jake. I told you I loved you and wanted to be with you." With that, he kissed Jake hard as the two men's arms enveloped one another again...and forever.

Loving Your Enemy

The day had finally arrived. Both men knew that it would and had been preparing for it all of their lives. They had both known of each other since they were young boys and had somehow sensed that, one day, they would come together in battle to settle the question of who, between them, was the mightiest gladiator of all time.

Both of them were respected and revered among the populace as well as being sought after by both male and female patrons who were only too willing to worship and satisfy both men's every whim and need.

Even the emperor himself was rumored to lust after the two men and determined that one or both of them would one day be by his side. Thus the reason for the contest that both men were being brought together for. Reasoning that his subjects would never permit even their leader to own both of them, the emperor announced to one and all that these two men would meet in combat and the winner would, indeed, become his property for all time.

Having been notified of the upcoming announced battle two months earlier, both men began training with increased zeal at their respective camps away from the city. No one was allowed in their camps except for their trainers and young men employed there.

Lucanus, from the northern province, had been looking forward to this day all of his life and was completely convinced that he could defeat his counterpart and win the favor of the emperor. At 6'3" and 285 pounds, his body was as if it had been sculpted from marble with not an ounce of fat anywhere on his frame. With his chiseled frame and handsome face, Lucanus was well aware of the looks and admiration that he attracted, although he had never used it to his advantage. His need to fight outweighed any other sort of need he had ever considered.

From the western province was Brocchus, equally as muscled and handsome, stood 6'4" and 290 pounds. He as well knew the admiration that he received each and every time he fought or was out in the marketplace but, like Lucanus, was driven by his need to fight above all else.

Both these powerful gladiators had battled their way to the top for many years, yet always knew that their ultimate battle was yet to be. Spies from both camps reported to both sides that these two men were training and pushing themselves beyond anything that had come before. Whoever came out the winner of this combat would, indeed, be the envy of the land for the rest of their lives and beyond.

As the time drew closer and closer, the emperor could not resist paying visits to the two camps to see for himself how ready these two warriors were. By day, both Brocchus and Lucanus trained from sunup to sundown. At night, the two men were locked away in lavish rooms and were fed and watered to their satisfaction.

Both their bodies were at the peak of perfection and both of them were ready to meet on the appointed day. Neither man was allowed any kind of sexual activity whatsoever and, in fact, the emperor had ordered that both men's manhoods be confined so that they could not engage in any kind of sex.

This, however, did not stop either of them from thinking about the other at night alone in their rooms. Both Brocchus and Lucanus dreamed about their battling one another before their emperor and this never failed to stimulate them while they slept. Their need to fight each other quickly became a lusting need to own one another in the arena, with only one man surviving.

Both of them soon realized that there was more to their passion than just the fight. As if they were of one mind, the two gladiators soon realized that there were deeply-buried feelings of lust for one another as well which they could do nothing about. Believing that these feelings grew out of their need to fight one another, they used the feelings to train harder and more intensely than ever before.

In the week prior to the combat, both of them had been locked away one night after a long, hard day of training and, as ordered, their manhoods were bound and confined so as to keep their enforced celibacy intact.

That night, Lucanus slept fitfully inside his room, waking several times in a cold sweat as thoughts of battling his opponent raged through his mind, his confined manhood throbbing and pulsing.

Brocchus, as well, lay awake thinking only of the upcoming battle and suffering the same pain in his loins. He somehow knew that his competitor was experiencing the same feelings and he felt as though his body would explode without some kind of release.

Knowing that the trainers checked on him regularly throughout the night, Brocchus devised a plan so that he could leave his room without their realizing it. He knew that tonight was the night that he had to get away, even for an hour or so to satisfy his urges. Waiting until he was alone in his room, the gladiator assembled the skins and ropes together that he had collected and arranged them beneath the heavy blankets he slept under so that when the trainers looked in, they would assume that he was fast asleep.

As he finished this, he heard the outer door of the compound open, alerting him that one of them was coming by to check on him. Making sure that his deception was well-laid out, he moved toward the back of his room and pulled out the heavy stone that he had spent a week trying to work loose so that he could escape undetected.

The stone pulled away freely and Brocchus climbed into and slid through the opening, pulled the stone back in place once he was through. Placing his ear to the stone wall, he heard the trainer stop at the door of his room and say, "Sleep well, gladiator. Victory will soon be at hand."

Smiling to himself as he realized his deception had indeed worked, Brocchus moved quietly away from the camp toward the cool sands of the desert, his hands already tugging and untying the confining bonds restricting his groin. The moon was full that night as he kept looking back to ensure he had not been followed.

As he climbed to the top of a small dune and started down the other side, suddenly he stopped short as he realized that someone was coming over from the opposite side of the dune. Crouching down and hoping not to be seen, Brocchus waited and watched as the figure moved down the side of the dune into the flat area, looking constantly over their shoulder.

The figure came toward the center of the flat area as the bright moonlight shone down. With a quiet gasp, Brocchus realized that it was Lucanus standing there. Quickly realizing the situation, it seemed as if he was not the only one who had needed to escape for a night. His mind racing as to if he should reveal himself or not, the gladiator suddenly realized that his unbound manhood was standing at its full length and that his hand was around it, stroking it as he watched his competitor in the moonlight.

Lucanus looked around again to ensure no one had followed him as his hands worked the binds holding his manhood in place. As the last strand came loose, his thick manhood jutted out, hard and proud in the night. He smiled to himself as he wrapped one muscular fist around it and began working it up and down, wanting, needed this relief and time to himself.

Brocchus watched, holding his breath, his mouth salivating at the sight of Lucanus standing there in the moonlight giving himself pleasure. His own manhood throbbing harder and harder as his hand kept working it while he watched, suddenly he knew that they were both here by fate.

Raising up to his feet, Brocchus moved forward across the sand toward Lucanus, who hearing the footsteps, stopped what he was doing and looked up, a quiet gasp leaving his mouth.

Neither man said a word as they both stood there facing one another, their muscled bodies bathed in the bright moonlight. Their eyes met and locked together, both realizing in an instant how they had come to meet here and both knowing that if they were caught, the punishment would be death.

Lucanus broke the silence as he whispered to his competitor, "This is fate that we should meet here." Brocchus nodded in agreement as the gladiator asked, "It is not hate that drives us toward one another, is it?

The other man shook his head, replying, "No, it is not. But, we have no chance of escaping from the task before us."

His competitor came toward him, gripping the man's muscular biceps tightly as he said, "It is possible...if we work together and not apart." Brocchus gave Lucanus a questioning look as the man said, "I do not want to fight you or harm you any more than you want to do the same to me. We two are one and we have always known that. If you are willing, we can leave this place forever and start over... together."

The words hit Brocchus like a broadsword as he realized that the gladiator was right. He did not want to fight the man. He wanted and needed to love the man instead. His voice a low whisper, he said, "I am willing. But, we must do it quickly before we are discovered."

Lucanus nodded his head in agreement, then said, "There is time, my beloved. First, however..." With that, both men reached down, wrapping a fist around each other's throbbing manhoods at the same time, working them furiously, both knowing that they needed the release that they'd been denied for so long. Their muscular bodies shone in the moonlight as they pumped and stroked each other faster and faster until, gasping as quietly as possible, both men emptied their seed onto the cool sands at their feet.

By the following morning, both gladiators were miles away from their respective camps, having taken horses, clothing and supplies while their trainers slept on. They'd decided to travel on until they reached a land where they were unheard of to begin their new life together. They both knew what would happen to the trainers when the emperor discovered that they'd left, but it was a small price to pay for ensuring both their futures.

After weeks of travel, the two former gladiators reached a new land and were relieved when none of the populace recognized them. They soon obtained citizenship and jobs in their new home and living quarters as well.

Their first night together in their new home, Brocchus held Lucanus in his arms as he said, "What is that old proverb about 'loving your enemy'?"

The man in his arms smiled and replied, "Yes, and the enemy loves you too."

A Boner Book

Never Farther Than Your Front Door

"Here it is, Friday night, and I'm sitting here in front of the TV with nothing better to do! Hmmph!" said the lanky, muscular man as he flipped through channels with the remote control. Dave Castillo was bored out of his mind and he knew it. Since retiring from the state college where he'd been coach of the varsity wrestling team, he had been spending far too many days and nights with too much time on his hands.

He had thought that once he retired, he would have time for all the plans and trips and projects that he'd thought about for many years, but when the day came, he found that retirement wasn't quite what he had expected to be.

Still, at forty-seven years of age, there were so many things he wanted to do and places he wanted to visit, but something kept preventing him getting up and doing something about it. Some days, he felt as though something kept telling him to just wait, that something was coming his way soon, but he shrugged that off as just wishful thinking.

The retired coach turned off the TV and threw the remote down on the coffee table. Standing up, he said to himself, "OK, Castillo, get your butt in gear and get out of this house. Cabin fever is no damn fun and I've got a bad case of it!"

Going to his bedroom, he changed out of the gym shorts and tank he was wearing into a pair of jeans, boots and a polo shirt. He had no idea where he was going or what he would do once he got there, but he knew he had to get out of there before the four walls got any closer than they already were. He grabbed his keys and went out to his SUV and got in, pulling out and heading toward the center of the small town. "Maybe just a good, long drive will help," he said to himself as he drove on.

———————

The sports car pulled into a parking space and came to a stop. The driver opened the door and got out, closing and locking it behind him as he made his way from the parking lot toward the video rental store ahead of him. Jon Brooks had moved back three weeks ago to the small town where he'd grown up. Leaving his home had been hard for him, but after that nasty divorce he'd gone through with his ex-wife, he desperately needed a change of scenery and a fresh outlook. He had no regrets about leaving the big city and the bad memories behind.

As he went inside the video store, he looked around to see if there was anyone he remembered. The small town was still the same as Jon remembered it and it felt good to be back there. His high school sweetheart and now-ex wife Joanna had pushed him to leave and he had only done it to please her. Moving into the video racks, he grinned and thought to himself, "Well, she can have the big city and all that B.S. Give me the small town life anytime." Jon moved on farther into the store, not really focusing on the titles of the videos as he glanced around, wondering if the store had an adult section.

―――――――――

Dave parked his SUV in the parking lot and got out, closing the door behind him. Turning around, he looked up at the brightly-lit sign on the front of the video store and grinned to himself, "I spend my time in front of the TV and where do I end up? A video store! As if I don't get enough mindless entertainment." He knew, however, that the store had a good adult section and from the tugging he felt between his muscled legs, he knew why he'd ended up there and what he was looking for.

As he entered the store, his eyes fanned around the store. Just then, he caught a glimpse of a man with sandy brown hair going into the back area where they kept the adult movies. Cocking his head, an old memory came back to him. Shrugging his shoulders, he thought, "Nah, couldn't be. Just my overactive imagination playing tricks on me again."

Pretending to look at the shelves of regular videos, Dave made his way toward the rear of the store. As he got to the entrance, he glanced back to see if anyone was looking, but realized that the store was empty except for the clerk at the front counter. Grinning to himself, the ex-coach went through the entrance and began looking through the shelves full of adult videos, absent-mindedly rubbing a hand against his bulge.

Remembering that he'd seen someone else come in here, he forced himself to stop doing that. "Time enough for that when I get home," he thought to himself.

He'd just passed the shelves stocked with straight adult movies and was turning the corner, headed for the gay section, when suddenly he ran into the other person, the two of them colliding together. "Ummpphhh," grunted Dave as he moved back and grabbed at the wall to steady himself.

The other man stumbled back a couple steps and mumbled a low "sorry" as he stooped down to retrieve the video he'd dropped on the floor.

Looking down at the man in front of him, Dave waited for him to stand up again. His jaw dropped open as he said, "Jon? Jon Brooks?"

The man in front of the coach looked up and replied with a shocked look on his face, "Coach? Coach Castillo? Oh my god!"

Sticking out a hand, Dave pumped Jon's hand as he said, "What the hell are you doing here?"

As the two men broke the handshake, the younger, shorter man replied, "Same as you, I guess, Coach." Realizing he was still holding the video in his hands, he quickly shoved it onto a nearby shelf and said, "I was just bored at home and thought I'd come in and get some entertainment."

Grinning, Dave said playfully, wagging a finger at the man, "Now now, young man. Don't you know this stuff will rot your brain?"

Jon returned the grin and said, "Well, if my brain hasn't rotted after all this time, I don't think there's much chance that'll happen soon."

The ex-coach chuckled at that as he said, "Always the smartass, aren't you, kiddo? Still, you were the best damn wrestler I ever coached at State. But, I thought you'd got married and moved off to the big city? How come you're back in town?"

The younger man said, "Thanks for that, Coach, but that was a long time ago. Why I'm back is a long story and this isn't really the kind of place to tell it."

Dave smiled and said, "Well, hell, I've got an idea. How about we get out of here and you come visit your old coach at his place? I only live a few miles away."

Jon grinned and replied, "Yeah, I remember where you live, Coach. Sounds like a better way to spend an evening than watching this crap for sure."

"Great," said Dave as he and the younger man exited the back room and made their way through the store out to the parking lot. Finding that they'd parked side by side, he said, "Now, that's just weird. Parked side by side. You'd think somebody planned this."

The younger man grinned at that as he unlocked and opened the door of his car. "Well, Coach, you always told me that we make our own destinies, so who knows, right?"

The ex-coach laughed at that as he went around to his vehicle telling his former student to follow him. As Dave drove away with his former student following, old memories came flooding back to him as he remembered watching his star wrestler as he struggled to push away the feelings that he knew were there but never to do anything about.

━━━━━━━━━━

Minutes later, the two men pulled up into the driveway of the large ranch house that Dave owned. As they got to the front door, the ex-coach said, "Just don't mind the mess. I'm not much of a housekeeper, kiddo."

Jon smiled as they entered the house. Dave motioned him over to the sofa in the living room as he closed the door behind him.

The ex-coach went to the kitchen coming back with two bottles of water for them and sat down in the large recliner next to the sofa. The two men began talking and catching up on everything that had happened since the younger man had married and moved away. After taking a drink from his bottle, Dave asked, "So, how come you came back, Jon? I thought you and...Joanna, isn't it? were headed for the big city and better things."

The younger man half-grinned and replied, "Well, that was the plan alright, Coach. But, once we got there, I found out she liked the big city life...a helluva lot better than I did."

Dave said, "Ah, parties every night, huh? Too much, too fast?"

Jon said, "Well...she had the parties actually. A different man every day and every night, while I was out busting my ass working. When I found out, I sued her for divorce and would you believe, the bitch laughed and said she never had any intention of us staying together? Told me I was just her meal ticket out of here."

The ex-coach frowned and said, "Well, I'm sorry to hear about that, man. Never been married myself, but who knows? The right person might come along some day."

Jon smiled at that and said, "Well, that's my story, Coach. What've..."

Dave interrupted him and said, "OK, first things first, Jon. We aren't at State anymore. You can call me Dave, unless you feel more comfortable calling me Coach."

The younger man grinned and said, "That's cool...Coach Dave. So, what've you been doing lately? You said you finally retired from State. How's the team doing there, by the way?"

The older man replied, "Well, since I retired, I haven't been doing much really. I've got a lot of ideas about doing things around here and traveling, but I haven't done anything about them. Last I heard, the team is doing OK." He stopped to take a drink of water and said, with a satisfied smile, "Of course, the team today isn't nearly as good as it was when you were my star wrestler and I was coaching."

Jon had the decency to blush at the compliment and said, "Thanks, Co...Dave. Yeah, those were the good old days alright. By the way, there's always been something I wanted to ask you, but never got the nerve to."

Dave swallowed, wondering what his former student was about to ask. Thinking to himself, he said, "Nah, he wouldn't ask that. I've never given anybody reason to know about the real me." Taking another swallow of water, he said, "What's that, Jon?"

The younger man said, "Well, when I was on the team, I always heard the other guys talking about you bringing them here and putting them through a rough one on one workout...rougher than we got on the mats, I mean. What's the story there?"

The ex-coach smiled and replied, "I guess good news travels fast, huh? It's true I did have some of the team over one for one on one training and sometimes the action got a bit rougher than on the mats at school, but I only did that with the ones that needed..." He stopped suddenly as Jon looked at him with a hint of sadness in his eyes and the beginning of a frown on his face. Dave moved forward in his recliner and said, "What the matter, man? You asked about that and..."

Jon said, "Yeah, I know. I was wondering if that really happened...and how come you never..."

Before he could finish, the ex-coach knew what he was going to say. "How come I never had you over for one of those workouts?" The younger man nodded as Dave answered, "I only did those workouts for the guys that really needed to improve, Jon. You never needed anything like that. You were my star wrestler and I knew I could always count on you to give your very best every time."

"Thanks, Dave, I appreciate that. I worked hard to never try and let you down, you know." Letting a quiet sigh escape, he went on. "But, from what I heard the other guys saying, it sounded like those workouts were a lot of fun. I thought about asking you if I could come over for one of those, but..."

The older man interrupted, saying, "...but you thought I'd would've said no, don't you?" Taking another drink of his water, he said, "Hell, Jon, if I thought you'd needed that, I would've had you over ahead of all the rest of them." Looking in the younger man's eyes, he said, "I guess I just it never occurred to me that you might want to do that. I'm sorry I never had you over for one of those workouts, man. I should've realized that my star pupil would want that. You would've been great at that, too."

Jon half-grinned at the apology and the compliment, saying, "It's cool, Dave. I probably should've come right out and asked. From what the other guys said, those workouts sounded like they got pretty damn rough and hot."

Blinking at the younger man's last word, Dave's mind raced as he thought, "Is he trying to tell me something? Or am I reading too much into it?" Bringing his attention back to his guest, the ex-coach said, "Well, from what I can see, Jon, you look like you've kept yourself in shape since school. And, I'd like to think I've still got what it takes, so, what do you say? Would my star wrestler like to join his old coach in my mat room for one of my private, intensive workouts?"

Before he could finish, Jon was smiling and nodding his head up and down. "Hell yeah, Coach! I mean Dave. I always wanted one of those and I'd love it!"

Getting up out of the recliner, Dave said, "Well, OK then! But, I think you might want to change out of your street clothes for it and get into some gear?" Jon looked down at himself, then looked back up and was about to say something when the ex-coach said, "I know...you don't have any gear with you. That's not a problem. I kept some of the extra singlets that got ordered for the team...sort of as a memento, I guess. I'm sure there's one that'll fit you." As his former pupil stood up as well, he said, leading the man out of the room and down the hall, "C'mon, kiddo. Let's go get geared up and hit the mats."

Both men stood opposite each other in Dave's converted mat room that was covered in thick wrestling mats from wall to wall and hanging from the walls as well. The ex-coach had given Jon a light green singlet that fit him like a second glove. The fact that the younger man's bulge stood out did not escape Dave's attention, who was geared up in a white singlet that hugged his hairy, muscular body just as well. They'd agreed to forego wearing jocks under them and it was evident that they were both turned on and looking forward to this.

As they stretched out on the mats, the older man said with a smirk on his face, "Hope you're ready to get your butt kicked by your old coach, kiddo."

Jon grinned back as he said, "No problem, Coach. I'll go easy on you. So, what style are we going for here? Collegiate rules? Freestyle? What exactly?"

Dave got to his feet at the same time as his former student and said, "How about collegiate rules with some freestyle and roughhousing mixed in. Just go for it and see what happens." He threw a grin and wink at Jon as he said, "Just don't work your old coach over too hard, kiddo."

The younger man laughed and replied, "I'll try not to... but I don't know, the way those guys used to talk about it I might need to!"

As the two men began circling one another, looking for the lockup, Dave thought to himself, "This man is hotter than I remember in college. I'm going to have to keep my mind on what I'm doing for sure."

Suddenly, the ex-coach lunged into his opponent, getting behind him and, wrapping his arms around the man's waist, lifted him up off the mats and brought him down fast as he snaked his legs around Jon's keeping them trapped and spread apart.

Not having wrestled competitively in several years, the younger man groaned out as he was taken down fast, his ex-coach on top of him trapping his legs. He struggled underneath the man, working to find a way to escape.

As Dave lay on top of Jon, he felt his bulge throbbing and began to enjoy the momentary feeling of it shoved into the younger man's singlet-clad butt cheeks. He could feel Jon under him struggling to escape and knew he could do it as he quickly pulled away from his opponent and rolled back up to his feet. Grinning as Jon rolled away and stood again, Dave said, "Not bad for your old coach, huh, kiddo?"

His opponent grinned with a smirk and said, "No, not bad... but don't be getting cocky yet... we're just getting started..."

Just then, Jon charged into Dave and grabbed onto his head, grinding the man's face into his side with one arm, then quickly flipped him over and down to the mats, keeping the headlock cranked on tight.

Grunting from the pressure around his head, the ex-coach twisted around into his opponent and brought a forearm up fast, driving it between the man's legs up into his bulge. Jon gasped out from that and let go of Dave's head, moving away holding his now-aching bulge. Sucking in air, the younger man said, "Hey... I thought this was going to be a friendly little match, Coach?"

Dave looked at his former student with a smirk on his face as he replied, "What's the matter, Jon? Can't handle it, kiddo?" He also noticed that the younger man's bulge seemed to grow bigger after that low blow and felt his own cock twitching in response. Moving in again, Dave taunted his former star and said, "This ain't college no more, man. This is just you and me. Bring it on, college star!"

The younger man locked his eyes on his opponent's and shot back. "You're right... this ain't college..." Grabbing the straps of his singlet, Jon stripped them down off his shoulders, letting the top of the singlet drop down to his waist and said, "I'll bring it to you..." Charging in again, he locked up with his opponent and began shoving and pushing him across the room until he had slammed Dave against the wall, then drove a knee to his abs. Moving back, he brought an arm and clubbed him across the man's hairy, muscular chest. Backing away, Jon said, grinning, "How's that, Coach?"

Dave groaned out loud from his former student's attack. Sucking in air, he said, "Well, well, well, the college star likes to get rough too, I see." Mirroring Jon's action, the ex-coach stripped his singlet straps off his shoulders and arms and down to his waist as he said, "Fine by me, tough man." Not waiting for a response, he came at his opponent fast, landing a fast forearm to the side of his head, followed by a knee to his abs. Grabbing onto the younger man's head, he twisted them around fast, taking Jon down to the mats. Rolling onto his man, Dave straddled the younger man's chest and grinned down at him and said, "How's that, big man? Tough enough for you? You ready to submit now, kiddo?"

Jon suddenly became aware of the man's hairy, sweaty body on top of him, that bulge inches away from his face. Gasping for air, the younger man looked up into Dave's face and said, "In your dreams...old man."

Before Dave could react, the younger man reached up with both arms grabbing at the back of the ex-coach's neck and pulled his head down toward him. Suddenly, their eyes met again and before either of them knew what was happening, their mouths met in a hard, rough kiss, their tongues wrestling against one another.

Both men grunted and growled in surprise, but neither of them made a move to break apart as Dave slid his sweaty body down on top of Jon's, his hands coming up and holding onto the younger man's head as the kiss became harder and deeper. The two men's bodies molded and melded together, their hands began roaming each other with complete abandon, every inch of their flesh a new and unknown place for them to explore. Their moans and grunts echoed throughout the room as they began rolling around the room locked together by their arms and the kiss that became even harder and rougher. They had become two male animals lost in rut together.

Finally breaking the kiss, Dave raised up over the younger man with a frown on his face, then got up off of him to his feet. Reaching down, he grabbed onto one of Jon's hands, helping him to his feet. Turning away, his cock obviously hard as hell in his half-stripped singlet, the ex-coach said, "I...don't know...what just... happened, man...but..."

Jon got his breath back as he looked down at the tent in his singlet and grinned. Coming up behind the older man, he brought his arms up and around the man's waist, coming to rest as he pulled Dave against him and said, "I know what happened, Coach. I always knew you were gay and hell, I've lusted after you ever since my first day on the team." He turned Dave around, who had a shocked, but happy look on his face as the younger man said, "I knew after I left town that what I really wanted was waiting for me back here. I was too stupid to..."

Dave couldn't believe what he was hearing. This young man that he'd felt an instant attraction to from day one was telling him everything he had always wanted to say, but couldn't. He looked deep into the younger man's eyes, seeing and feeling the love in them. Smiling, the ex-coach kissed Jon again and said, "No, not stupid, kiddo. You always knew how to go after and get what you wanted. And, I always dreamed and fantasized that I'd be one of those goals of yours."

Jon smiled and said, "I love you Co...Dave. I guess I always have. That's the biggest reason I came back...to come looking for you. I had to find out for myself if what I felt was real or not."

Feeling as though an enormous weight had suddenly been lifted, Dave held Jon against him in a hug and felt the young man's arms hug him back tightly, the smile on Jon's face pressing against Dave's sweaty chest. Whispering gently, the older man said, "I love you too, kiddo. I know I always have and always will." Feeling the grin against his chest, Dave suddenly scooped the younger man up in his arms and headed toward the door of the room. Jon reached out opening the doorknob as he was being carried out, both of them knowing they were headed for the bedroom together as the ex-coach said, "Just like I've always told you kids. Never go looking too far for your dreams...farther than your own front door."

A Boner Book

Under The Waves

The sensation of being under the ocean was one that never failed to thrill Jim. In the fifteen years that he had been deep sea diving, each time was just as exciting and new as the first time. Each dive that he made was something like a new journey to him and the time he spent under the waves brought him a kind of peace and serenity he had never found on land.

He usually dived with his friends, however, this morning he was in the mood for some solitude and arrived at his favorite dive area alone, feeling more exhilarated today than he ever had. The morning sun shone brightly over him and the boat as he quickly stripped down naked and began to strap on his diving gear, deciding to dive au natural. He loved the sensation of his naked body in the water and under the ocean and it never failed to give him a raging erection.

Placing his breather into his mouth, Jim sat down on the edge of the boat and rocked backwards over the side. The cold chill of the water was quickly replaced with a familiar warmth as his body was enveloped by the ocean. Looking up, he could still see the sun shining down atop the water, then he turned his body and began diving down into the depths.

Jim made his way carefully down through the water, knowing where the coral reefs were located from experience as he dived deeper and deeper. Keeping an eye on his air tank, the diver proceeded deeper down, feeling relaxed and calm. He knew this area well and watched the different types of sea life moving around and past him as he worked his way through the water.

Remembering an underwater grotto on one of his previous dives, Jim headed for it and soon was pulling himself up from the water. The above water area had always fascinated him. He thought of this place as his as he pulled his breather from his mouth and looked down at the water nearby, his naked body pulsing with excitement.

He unlimbered his tank from his back and decided to relax for awhile before heading back to the surface. Jim laid down on the cool rocks, enjoying the feeling of solitude and peace, his eyes drowsy. Before he'd realized it, he was fast asleep, the cool air and warm water all around him.

In his mind, he began to hear a faint voice calling to him, "Come...join me...I am waiting for you." The voice began to get louder until it seemed it was next to him and Jim awoke with a start, looking around for where the voice was coming from.

Seeing nobody there, he smiled to himself, saying, "Must have dreamed that...but it sure seemed real."

He sat up on the rocks and turned away from the water to get his tank when suddenly he heard the voice again. "I am here. Come and join me."

Turning back around toward the sound, Jim's jaw dropped open as his eyes widened. At the water's edge was the head and upper torso of the most beautiful man he had ever seen. He had blue-black long hair that draped down across his muscled shoulders that led to the kind of sculpted body one usually only saw in a museum.

The man smiled at Jim as he said, "I apologize for startling you, but I was passing by and saw you on the rocks. I have never seen others of my kind like you before."

Jim recovered his senses and replied, "I...thought what I'd heard was in a dream. I thought I was alone down here." Thinking about what this handsome man had just said, the diver said, "What did you mean when you said 'others of my kind'?"

Smiling again, the man replied, pointing to Jim's flippered feet, "You are a resident of the oceans, are you not? I have never seen any others with those before."

Jim looked down at his feet and said, "You mean my flippers? They're not...I mean, they're part of my diving equipment." Reaching down, he removed the rubber flippers to reveal his feet. "See? I'm a man...from above the ocean."

The man looked at Jim in amazement then back at his feet and said, "Oh! I did not know! You're a...a...land dweller?"

The diver replied, "Well, yes...if you mean I live on land, then yes...but, aren't you?"

The handsome man at the water's edge frowned slightly, then said, "No, I don't. Let me show you." Turning his body sideways, the lower half of his body came up out of the water.

Jim gasped in sudden surprise as he saw that the man's lower body ended in what appeared to be the lower half of the body of a fish, with a large fin where his feet ought to be. "You're a...a... merman?" he asked with a smile.

"Yes, I am," the dark haired man replied. "And you are a... human?" Jim nodded at that as the man lowered his fin back into the water. Propping his muscled arms onto the rock edge, he said, "I am called Aguan."

The diver replied, "I am called Jim." He stared at the man for a moment longer, then said, "Are you sure I'm not dreaming? I thought that people of the sea were just a fantasy...a dream."

Aguan's deep blue eyes met Jim's as he said, "No, you are not dreaming, Jim. We do exist here and we are real. Perhaps it is you who are the fantasy, however."

Jim grinned at that comment and said, "Touché, Aguan."

The merman smiled back as he looked at the man from head to toe, then said, "Do all of the land dwellers look like you?"

The diver looked down at his nude body, then back up at Aguan and said, "Well, usually we aren't naked. On land, we wear clothing or some kind of outer garment to conceal our bodies."

Aguan thought for a moment and replied, "How very odd, indeed. Why would anyone want to conceal their natural state?"

Jim laughed at that and said, "For the life of me, at the moment, I can't imagine a good answer for that." He grabbed his flippers pulling them onto his bare feet again and said, "Well, I should be returning to the surface. I have only enough air to make it back up there."

Aguan watched with fascination as Jim strapped the tank onto his back. As the diver stood up on the rocks and came forward, the merman said, "Will you return here again, Jim?"

The diver smiled down at the man at the rocks' edge and replied, "I'd like that, Aguan. Will you be here when I do?" he asked as he sat down on the edge of the rocks.

In reply, the merman raised up toward Jim, their eyes locking together. Their mouths came together in a hard kiss as the diver felt

126

Aguan's muscled arms enveloping his body, pulling him off the rocks and against his chiseled body.

━━━━━━━━

For weeks, Jim could think of nothing but his encounter with Aguan. At night and home alone, he would satisfy himself by recalling the merman and the adventure they had shared that day. He knew that the undersea resident wanted him to return, but Jim was somehow hesitant and slightly afraid of what would happen if he paid another visit to the grotto.

He resolved not to allow himself to give in to the desire that he felt, feeling that it would overwhelm him. Common sense told Jim that he didn't belong in Aguan's world anymore than the merman could exist in his world. Yet, there was something that pulled and called at Jim. Some long-buried feeling that he found ravenously tempting as well as overwhelmingly frightening about it.

━━━━━━━━

Day after day, Aguan visited the undersea grotto, hoping that the land dweller would return. Their time together had been one of the happiest times that the merman could remember and he suspected that Jim felt the same way. No one else of his kind had ignited and stirred the emotions and feeling that he was having.

After visiting the grotto again, the merman thought to himself, "Why, then, has the human not returned? Did I do something to frighten or insult him?" As he swam away, Aguan thought that the feelings that he was having would envelope him if the man never returned. If only he could be more like Jim, perhaps that would bring him back. If only...

===============

As he steered the boat out through the water, Jim's mind argued back and forth as he tried to make sense of all of it. Why was he going back to seek out the merman? What was it about Aguan that made it impossible for him to forget their encounter? How would the merman react should they meet again? Was he experiencing the same feelings that Jim was?

He dropped the anchor into the water and stood there, watching it sink below the depths. Still questioning his reasoning for being here, Jim stripped down and strapped on his diving gear and dropped back into the water. With each stroke of his arms and legs, he could somehow sense that the merman was nearby somewhere and the feeling was becoming stronger the nearer he got to the grotto.

Finally, he arrived at the recessed rocks and pulled himself from the water, pulled off his gear and laid it down. Jim sat down on the rocks near the water's edge and looked into the water, waiting for...what? He had no idea if Aguan would return or when he would. He had told himself that it all had to be a dream, but he had never experienced a dream as real and as vivid as what had happened that day.

Jim became lost in his thoughts when suddenly there was a ripple in the water, followed by a splash as Aguan emerged from the surface with a huge smile on his handsome face. "You came back!" exclaimed the merman.

The human smiled back as he said, "Yes, I told you I would, Aguan. I...don't know...why...but I had to return. I tried to stay away, but I couldn't."

His arms propped on the rocks' edge, the merman looked into Jim's eyes and replied, "You are not alone in that, Jim. I, too, don't know why but I could not stay away either. I have been back here many times looking and waiting for you."

Jim felt a well of emotions rushing through him as he said, "Aguan, we come from such different worlds. How can we expect to be together? You can't live out of the water and I certainly can't live under it, except for here. Are we expecting too much of each other?"

The merman looked deep into the human's eyes as he replied, "I understand what you are saying, but we both know that we have to be together. I cannot exist without you in my life and I think you feel the same way."

Jim moved closer to the water's edge and, in answer, dropped into the water, hugging Aguan against him as both man and merman became lost together in their mutual lust and love for one another.

====================

In what seemed like a millennium to him, Jim felt himself swept away as if he were riding a tidal wave. Suddenly, he felt himself awaken with a start. Images and sounds were flying past him in a blur until, at last, they began to slow and coalesce in his mind.

Opening his eyes which had hadn't realized were closed, he realized with a start that he was under the water and...he was breathing? Panic flew through him for a moment then he heard a familiar voice followed by the familiar feeling of Aguan's body against his. "Do not be alarmed, Jim." began the merman. "We are together now, as one."

Jim looked down into the depths and gasped as he saw that his lower body was now that of a merman's. His legs had been replaced with a large fin not unlike Aguan's. He raised his head up to look at the merman's as he tried to process what had happened.

In answer, the merman said, "You asked how we could be together. Now, we can be. Together. Forever." Taking one of Jim's arms, Aguan said, "Come. Let me show you our new home." The two merman swam off together through the depths...their life together just beginning.

The Escape

True to his word, John completed his report and submitted it to the commanding officer before leaving that evening. He'd worded it in such a way that nothing of what he'd experienced with Cairon was included. The commander had been unhappy that the scientist had not made much progress but accepted the report, thanking him for his efforts.

Later that evening, John was at home relaxing in bed, reading a book, but not really paying attention to it. His mind kept drifting to the day's events. Suddenly, he gasped as he heard a familiar voice inside his mind saying, "No! They cannot do this! John Fletcher! Please help me! I am in danger!"

Throwing the book aside, the scientist jumped out of bed and quickly dressed, not really understanding what had happened or why he was reacting like this. As he raced toward his front door, he heard something fall against it from the outside. As John grabbed the door knob, he heard a loud moan and yanked it open fast. The alien visitor fell against him, obviously in pain and suffering. "Cairon!" said John, "what in the world? What's happened? How did you get here?"

He felt the alien's mind connecting to his again as a painful voice responded, "Doctors...tried to...stimulate my brain...some kind of...device...had to...get away...had to...escape...had to...find... you..." With that, the man broke the connection and slipped into unconsciousness in the scientist's arms.

John's mind was racing as he lifted the alien up in his arms, the man still clad in what he could only describe as an opaque uniform of some kind, and carried him into the bedroom, laying him down on his bed. Grabbing his medical bag, the scientist checked for the alien over for any signs of threatening damage. Relieved that there didn't seem to be any permanent injury, he put his bag away and came over to the side of the bed, sitting down beside his unexpected guest.

Cairon lay there, his eyes closed as his chest rose and fell, breathing, John hoped, normally. Thinking for a moment, the scientist wondered if the alien had been followed, hopeful that no one had traced him here. Considering his next action for a moment, he said to himself, "If he can initiate contact with me, maybe I can do the same with him and find out what happened."

Looking at the man's face, John focused his mind trying to make contact with the alien. For a moment, it didn't seem to work when suddenly, the darkness came followed by the light again and knew their minds were connected. A quiet voice began speaking, "John? John Fletcher? You are here. I knew you would help me."

The scientist replied, "Yes, I'm here, Cairon. You are at my house...the structure in which I live. Tell me what happened. How did you escape and know where to come to find me?"

The voice becoming stronger now, John could hear in his mind as the alien responded, "Your...medical...staff...tried to stimulate my brain in order to force communication. Their machinery burned out with the attempt. I...what is the word you have?...falsified being unconscious. They left me in the room alone while they went to repair their machine. As soon as they were gone, I...you would call it...disintegrated my physical body and sent it out in search of you, John Fletcher. I had just completed reintegration at your...structure when you found me."

The scientist tried to comprehend what the alien was saying as he said, "You mean your people have the ability to project your bodies by a single thought anywhere that you want?"

Cairon responded. "Yes, we have that ability, but are only able to do that with others with whom we've connected mentally. On my planet, it is a common practice since we are all connected all the time. Since you were the only one of your people that I have connected with, I knew that I would find you."

John smiled as he saw the alien's eyes open finally, although they still communicated non-verbally. Explaining, the scientist said, "The doctors were most likely using a magnetic resonance imaging system on you. It's not a way of stimulating conversation, but rather it's a way of creating a three-dimensional cross-section diagram of part of a person...their brain, for instance, and, unfortunately, your brain."

The alien replied, "I understand now. From what I have assimilated from our earlier connection, I must assume that your people will come looking for me soon."

The scientist said, "You're right about that, Cairon. Obviously, you can't stay here. Since I work at the base, this will be one of the places they will search. But, where will you go? Your craft is under locked security on the base and I don't know if it was damaged when you crash landed here."

Suddenly, the alien broke the mental connection. John flinched less this time as Cairon said, "I must try and get back to my ship and leave your world, John Fletcher. It is much too dangerous for me to remain here and much too dangerous for you as well. I cannot allow any harm to come to you."

The scientist got up off the bed as the alien sat up slowly, having recovered at last. Thinking quickly, John said, "I could try hiding you in my car...my mode of transportation and get you inside the base, but I don't have the security override codes for where your craft is being stored."

Just then, there was a loud knock on the front door. Both of them looked at each other as Cairon said, "It is them. You must answer the door or it will raise suspicion, John Fletcher. Do not worry about me. I will remain hidden until they have gone."

Unsure about leaving the alien alone, John left the bedroom, closing the door behind him. He went to the front door, opening it as he rubbed at his eyes, giving the impression that he'd been asleep. The two security officers standing there looked at the scientist as one of them asked, "Dr. Fletcher? Sorry to wake you, sir, but there's been a security breach at Langley. Have you heard or seen anything unusual here tonight?"

Yawning widely for their benefit, John replied, "No, gentlemen. I've been here ever since I left the base around six tonight. I've been working on some lab reports for tomorrow, but I haven't seen or heard anything out of the ordinary. Can you tell me what you're looking for?"

The second officer replied, "No sir, we aren't allowed to say. This was one of the places we were ordered to check out. If you do notice anything strange, you should contact base security as soon as possible."

John nodded and said, "Of course. You have my word on that. I'll call in if I see anything strange, gentlemen. Now, if you'll excuse me, I have a long day tomorrow and need some rest."

The officers nodded and left as the scientist closed the door behind them, locking it back. He went back to the bedroom to find Cairon sitting on the bed. "A most convincing falsification, John Fletcher. They are placated for the time being. However, I do not think they will fail to return again."

Coming over as the alien stood up, the scientist said, "Let's wait a few minutes, then I'll get you in my car and take you on the base. After we're there, you'll be on your own, Cairon. I wish I could help more, but it's the best I can do."

The alien smiled and replied, "You have been of more help than you know, John Fletcher. I must try and leave your world before any more problems happen, however."

The scientist said, "Let's get going then, my friend. The sooner we get you back there, the better for you."

Cairon moved into the living room with John and said, "One question, however. Your vehicle. As your security personnel are on alert, are they not likely to search any vehicle coming out of or onto your base?"

The scientist frowned as he said, "Yes, you're right. They will be on high alert and search anyone and everyone. But, how else can we get you back, Cairon?"

The alien looked at the man with his dark eyes and said, "There is an alternative solution, but I am unsure whether or not you would be able to...what is the word?...handle it?"

John replied, "Tell me what it is! If there's another way to get you back undetected, I'm willing to do it. That's what's important right now."

Coming toward the scientist, Cairon reached out with his mind, connecting with John again and said, "It is time, my friend. Do not be alarmed. I have never attempted this with anyone other than my own people, but it should work."

Responding with his mind, John started to say, "Attempted what, Cai..." Suddenly, the scientist saw the bright light connecting their minds expand and contract bigger and bigger. The room around them began to dissolve, but then John realized it wasn't the room that was dissolving. It was he and Cairon! The alien was disintegrating them together and attempting to transport them onto the base.

John felt a sudden empty, sickening feeling as his body was reduced to atoms, but still felt the connection between their brains. Just as quickly, that empty feeling disappeared as he suddenly found himself standing there facing the alien outside of the security hangar that was holding Cairon's spacecraft.

The scientist stumbled and slumped against the alien, gasping for breath at being reintegrated for the first time. Cairon said, "I am again sorry, John Fletcher. It was the only way that I could see to solve our problem. You are unharmed?"

Finding his voice and realizing that their minds were not connected, John said, gasping, "Yes...yes...I'm...OK..." Hearing the sounds of boots pounding on the metal corridors and hallways around them, he said quickly, "It's all up to you now, Cairon. You have to get inside this structure. Your craft is behind these doors. Hopefully still working. You have to hurry before the others get here."

Moving John to one side, the alien looked at the electronic panel attached to the large hangar doors. Placing one hand against the panel, suddenly the display began running through random access codes until, at last, the lock uttered a loud chime and the doors began to roll open.

The sounds of the base security were getting closer as John shoved Cairon through the opening doors and shouted, "GO! Don't worry about me! You have to get out of here! I'll hold them off as long as I can!"

The alien moved inside the large hangar, his small spacecraft sitting there on its landing pads. Cairon made his way to the craft and, examining it, found it to be completely operational. Opening the hatch in the side, he started to climb in, then turned and said with his mind, "John Fletcher?"

Turning away from the approaching sounds, the scientist heard the alien in his mind and replied, "What, my friend?"

The alien smiled from across the hanger and said, "Come with me, John Fletcher. To my world. You would be welcomed there as an equal. I wish you to come with me." The scientist felt the confusion in the alien's thoughts as he struggled to think of the words he wanted. Then, Cairon said, "I need you, John Fletcher. With me. I...love...you."

The transferred thought nearly knocked the breath from the scientist as he sent back, "Cairon, you know that's not possible. I can't just disappear. You have to get away. I don't." Stopping for a moment, John heard the sounds getting nearer as the exterior doors began being unlocked. Looking back at the alien standing there, suddenly he knew what he had to do. Running at full speed toward the spacecraft, John said, "What the hell!"

The exterior doors opened suddenly and security personnel and armed soldiers began streaming in as Cairon grabbed onto John's arm, pulling him inside the craft as the men running in shouted out for both of them to move away from the spacecraft.

As they men raised their weapons, the alien pushed John through the hatch and into the craft, saying, "Do not worry, John Fletcher. They will not be able to harm us. Their weapons will prove useless." The hatch closed behind the alien and he pushed past the scientist toggling a sequence into a panel on the wall.

The scientist could hear the gunfire starting, then, surprisingly, the yells of the soldiers and security personnel as they began running in all direction, their fired ammunition deflecting back toward them.

Cairon's hands flew across the lighted panels. John was thrown back into a large padded chair against the wall as the craft powered up and began to raise up from the hangar floor. Turning toward the scientist, the alien sat down in what John assumed was a command chair and said, "Prepare yourself, John Fletcher. We are about to leave your world."

Not waiting for a response, the alien keyed in another sequence and suddenly John's last memory was of being flattened back against the chair he was in as the craft raised up and flew out of the hangar in the blink of an eye, rocketing away from the Earth toward space.

===============

Opening his eyes at last, the scientist felt groggy but rested as he moved his body, raising up on one elbow. As he did, Cairon said in his mind, "We are almost there, John. Welcome to your new home."

A smile spread across the scientist's face, followed by a sudden shock as he realized that both he and the alien were nude underneath some kind of blanket that conformed to their bodies as they laid together. Pulling his thoughts together, John said, "How long have we? I mean, you and I? We...together?"

Cairon smiled wider as he replied, "Yes, John. You and I... together. As we will be always...in a perfect world...a utopia."

About the Author

Dan lives in the beautiful surroundings of the mountains of western North Carolina with his family of three men and three cats in their three-story log home, nicknamed "The Treehouse", where he spends a good deal of his time pursuing his writing as well as reading any and everything he can get his hands on.

Dan counts the collected works of Agatha Christie as well as those of Greg Herren, Daniel Erickson, Matt Bernstein Sycamore, Patricia Nell Warren, John Grisham, Stephen King and the late Madeleine L'Engle among his favorite authors. His other passions are, besides writing, classic movies and television, graphic design and computers.

With his fourth book completed and being the true glutton for punishment that he is, Dan is already outlining and working on a fifth book which will be a full-scale science-fictional novel based on "A Meeting Of Minds" and "The Escape".

Dan is also the author of the *BLACKNBLUE Tavern* trilogy.

CARROLL

BLACK**N**BLUE
TAVERN

BLACKNBLUE TAVERN

book one of a trilogy by
Dan Carroll

A
BONER
BOOK

BLACK**N**BLUE
TAVERN

book two of a trilogy by
Dan Carroll

A BONER BOOK

CARROLL

BLACKNBLUE TAVERN

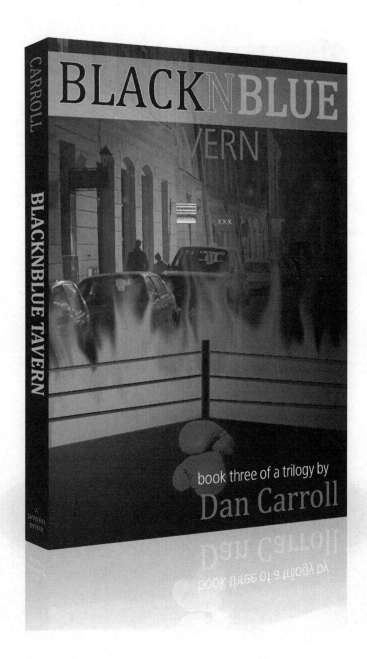